Heart Full of Rainbows

Heart Full of Rainbows

Melanie Randolph

Five Star
Unity, Maine

Copyright © 1983 by Melanie Randolph

All rights reserved.

Five Star Romance.
Published in conjunction with Toad Hall, Inc.

Cover photograph by Tom Knobloch.

October 1998
Standard Print Hardcover Edition.

Five Star Standard Print Romance Series.

The text of this edition is unabridged.

Set in 11 pt. Plantin.

Printed in the United States on permanent paper.

Library of Congress Cataloging in Publication Data

Randolph, Melanie.
    Heart full of rainbows / Melanie Randolph.
      p. cm.
    ISBN 0-7862-1597-6 (hc : alk. paper)
    I. Title.
PS3568.A555H43   1998
813′.54—dc21   98-8708

Heart Full of Rainbows

1

"It's not my turn. I walked the dog yesterday!"

Six-year-old Cindy's snippy voice, amazingly powerful considering the owner's mere forty pounds, boomed up the circular stairs, down the hall, across the study, and into Beth Columbine's bedroom, shoving her rudely awake. She winced and rolled over to face the bedside clock, which accused her of oversleeping by ten minutes as it flipped to 7:10. She wondered briefly where Joe was before she remembered he'd been gone for six weeks now, to Bantry House, Bellemonte's century-old hotel. The full-length mirror on their bathroom door reflected the stark, sudden pain of remembrance. Joe had always said her face was like a pretty kitten's. For an agonizing moment, she stared into a reflection of her own grief. Her eyes were huge and black, almost like obsidian disks, with little delineation between pupil and iris. Her chin was pointed, making her face seem heart-shaped. Joe called her Valentine.

Or Kitten. Or Baby.

She shut her eyes, refusing to fall into the trap of self-pity that she'd skillfully avoided for six weeks. For longer than that, really. Joe had been acting like a total jerk for months before they'd finally called it quits.

No use remembering, she thought determinedly, and turned her back to the mirror. She listened to the kids' usual early morning bickering until she was sure one of them had finally taken the pregnant beagle, Daisy, out for a walk.

Until Beth had started working for Professor Ternan eight

months ago, when the youngest of the three children had started first grade, walking Daisy had been her responsibility — although she was the only one in the family who hadn't wanted a dog. Joe had brought Daisy home as a puppy, saying he'd take care of her and train her to obey. Beth had laughed at that; Joe couldn't even train the kids to obey. He was too much of a pushover for anything small and cute.

But, of course, once the kids had seen the dog, there'd been no refusing to let them keep it. Although Beth was usually enough of a disciplinarian to balance Joe's overindulgence of the children, even she hadn't had the heart to separate them from the beagle pup with ears like daisy petals.

Naturally, Joe hadn't taken care of the dog, and Beth had had to until she'd started her job. Then she'd insisted the kids take turns walking and feeding Daisy. Joe was supposed to take her to the vet to be spayed, but, as with so many things she'd asked him to do, he just never got around to it. Now they were stuck with a pregnant beagle. No one had any idea how long she'd been pregnant. All they knew was that their pedigreed hound would be having a litter of pups whose parentage was as big a mystery as what had happened to Joe and Beth Columbine's model marriage.

Beth felt her solitariness in the big bed acutely. Mornings had been her most contented time. They'd usually wake up simultaneously. If she'd slipped from Joe's arms during the night, she'd grope her way sleepily back into them. Gradually they became aware of the luxury of shared warmth, of the morning light, of bird song coming through the partly opened window, of the kids' radios and laughter — of the magical world they'd built around themselves and their love.

They'd gotten married nine years ago. Joe had already completed college, but she'd only had two years. Still, he'd landed an excellent position with a real estate firm and had a five-thousand-dollar inheritance from his grandmother's estate. Both of their Italian families had approved of the marriage wholeheartedly. Certainly Beth couldn't blame their separation on marrying too young, as their friends tended to do. Joe had been twenty-five, and she'd been only twenty. He should have let her grow up first, their friends said.

She clenched her jaw angrily. Horse feathers! *He* was the child. *He'd* wanted to spend the five thousand dollars on a European honeymoon. It was she who'd insisted on making the down payment on the twelve-room Victorian house, tastefully divided into three apartments and located on a fine street. They'd had a steady income from two of the apartments during the early years when Kate, Josh, and Cindy had joined them one right after the other. Joe hadn't been very farsighted about that, either. After the third birth in three years, Beth's obstetrician had declared she might not be safe having another child. She'd had a difficult time with all of them, but particularly with Cindy. Joe had been sick at heart, blaming himself for making her the mother of three when she was still so young herself. He'd promised the obstetrician there'd be no more children and then taken the steps to ensure it.

Freed from childbearing and loving Joe and her children, Beth had been hectically happy. They had enough money so that, as their tenants moved out to their own homes, they weren't forced to relet the apartments. Their own family of five spread out and enjoyed the enormous, picturesque house. The children used the third-floor apartment as a playroom, its living room for television and games, its kitchen as a snack center. Although Joe was the first to admit that Beth had a far better business head than he did, he'd never let her handle their finances, declaring she had enough to occupy her time and attention with three small children and a behemoth of a house to care for. She'd wanted to continue renting at least the third-floor apartment, but Joe had declared grandly that it was only money and it was great to have the apartment empty for the kids and visiting relatives. The real estate business was booming, so she didn't argue.

She'd *never* argued with Joe, she realized. She adored him. Who wouldn't, for heaven's sake? He was absolutely the most wonderful man she'd ever met. Zorba the Greek, only properly domesticated. He was handsome and good, kind and loving, devoted to her and the children. Anything she'd ever wanted had been hers for the asking.

Until she'd gone back to college.

She clenched her fists against the blue candlewick bedspread. Even after all those months, the shock of Joe's reaction to her enrollment was so painful that tears prickled behind her eyelids. It wasn't as if her entering college had come as a total surprise to Joe; she'd talked of nothing else since they'd learned that Cindy would be the last child. Indeed, when they'd married, she'd talked about wanting to return to school one day. She'd been a dean's-list student at college, bright and with a flare for writing. She'd been developing this skill and studying medieval history, having wanted to write historical fiction ever since she'd discovered *Robin Hood* in the town library when she was ten years old. During all the years since she and Joe had met, through all the years of their marriage, she'd blithely assumed he approved of her desire for education. Certainly he'd never given her any reason to suspect he didn't. Whenever she spoke of college, he smiled and nodded in a complacent way.

Yet last summer, when she'd gone to enroll at the university, ten miles away, and had come home that evening to ask him to write a check for the fee, he'd suddenly turned her entire world upside down by declaring he wouldn't pay for her tuition, that he didn't think she ought to be considering leaving their children alone to pursue an education.

"But honey, I'm only taking morning classes," she'd protested. "I'll be home long before they are. And if I can't schedule all morning classes next term and can't be here when they get home from school, Jenny Krouse, their regular baby-sitter, will stay with them until you or I get home."

"See? Already you're planning to leave them alone."

"You never protest one bit when I leave them alone to go off on a business trip with *you!*" she'd retorted. "Mrs. Penniman stays with them for three days or more at a time."

"That's different. That's necessary."

She'd stared at him earnestly. "This is necessary to me, Joe," she'd said quietly. "I've dreamed of this for years. You never indicated you would mind."

"You never asked. I never said it was going to be okay with me."

"I don't believe this, Joe. Why shouldn't it be okay with you?"

"Because, Beth, we each have our jobs to do in this marriage. Mine is selling real estate, which isn't always easy to do. Nor is coping with a boss like Springfield. I need to know everything's okay at home. That you're here with the kids and that they're being well taken care of. As only you can, honey," he'd added, attempting to soften his opposition with the smile that usually made her knees weak and her heart ache with longing.

But this time she'd steeled herself against the sweet yielding to his will. Her dream of going to college, of learning to write historical fiction, was too dear, too strong to relinquish so easily.

"Are you implying that if I go to school, the children won't be taken proper care of? That, in short, I won't be doing my share of the work of this marriage?"

"Beth, you know very well that you're always deploring the way kids seem to be rearing themselves these days," he'd said evasively. "I just don't understand why you're willing to dump

11

our kids into the rat pack of unsupervised children."

That had done it.

Beth couldn't clearly remember all the things she'd shouted at him. Unreasonable, she'd called him. Selfish. Pig-headed. Chauvinist. Some even worse. But Joe was stubbornly unyielding. Once he'd even spent a night in jail rather than pay for a speeding ticket he swore he didn't deserve.

But a bitter anger she'd never dreamed she could feel against her adored husband came to life that day. The idea that he, who controlled the purse strings, would actually refuse her reasonable request for tuition as if she were a dependent, supplicating parasite infuriated her. A large part of their worldly goods were theirs because of her foresight. The money that had made the down payment on the house would long since have been converted to francs, pounds, and lira and gone into some *pensione* keeper's bank account if she hadn't insisted they buy the house. Then she'd set about filling it with sturdy furniture and antiques that she'd picked up for next to nothing at garage sales and auctions. Joe had scorned many of the pieces until she'd made them beautiful by removing coat after coat of paint and old varnish and reupholstering the couches and chairs. Then he had been lost in wonder at her unsuspected skill and pointed out to visitors with pride Beth's latest "project."

No, she'd never drawn a paycheck, but her thrift and skill had made a big contribution to their financial worth as a family. Even Joe admitted that if he'd allowed her to manage the checkbook, they'd be worth considerably more today.

Thinking of paychecks had taken her the next logical step.

When school had started, she'd simply applied for work at the university and been hired as a typist and unofficial editor for Professor Tim Ternan. If Joe refused to pay her tuition, she'd thought defiantly, she would earn the money herself.

To Joe's complete dismay, she had.

Beth rolled over on her back and stared at the ceiling. Despite her resolve not to cry, tears overflowed her eyes and made wet tracks into her hair. Now it was all over. Today they had an appointment with Judge John Willoughby, and, since Pennsylvania had no-fault divorce, they'd soon be part of each other's pasts. The thought filled her with anguish, but what else could she do?

It wasn't as if she didn't fully understand how very much she was losing in divorcing Joe. The thought of his dear face and voice made the tears come more quickly.

Nor was she unaware that a good part of the "fault" was hers. If she'd been content to lie down and play dead, if she'd crawled back under Joe's gentle thumb, she'd still be his cherished darling. He would still love her. She bit back hard on a great, welling sob. If she lived to be a hundred, she'd never forget that last horrible fight, the climax to so many battles which had begun after she'd started to work. Their marriage had seemed to end abruptly the night she'd shouted at him that he wouldn't be having so much trouble with her working and trying to improve herself if he truly loved her.

"I don't know if I *do* love you," he'd yelled.

His words had been like a bolt of lightning that had rent her heart.

"If we don't have love, then we don't have anything," she'd cried and, before either of them had quite recovered from the shock of his words, she'd asked him to leave. He'd stomped upstairs and packed a bag. He'd moved out that very night, his jaw set in what she'd come to call his "bulling look."

As she thought of that night, an all-too-familiar anger dried her tears. It was over. What love he'd ever felt for her had been of such a selfish variety as to be worthless, even to a hopeless romantic like her. He had not been content with her whole strength and health, with every waking and sleeping moment, with all, in fact, that she had to give him. He'd wanted her very soul, too. That's what he'd have finally gotten — a poor, whipped, worthless pigmy soul — if she'd allowed him to keep her from her heart's desire.

Today they'd end it. Today the unthinkable would occur. Fortunately the house was in both their names. When they sold it she'd get *something* after the mortgage was paid off. That was the law, her lawyer said. Although, to hear Joe talk, everything belonged to him. It was *his* house, *his* furniture, *his* money. She'd see how long his half would last. When they went out to dinner with another couple, he was always the first to grab the check. If a pretty dress in a store window took his eye, he'd go in and buy it, bringing it home to Beth, saying it looked as if it had been made just for her. No matter that it cost eighty dollars. The thought made her heart lurch painfully. *Dear Joe. Sweet Joe.* She almost cried again as she thought of all the years of joy, of laughter, of love.

All gone. All washed away the first time she wanted something for herself that *he* didn't want.

She threw back the sheet and bedspread and swung her legs to the floor. She couldn't put off starting the day any longer.

Her lawyer, an avowed feminist, was impressed with Joe's "decency." Although Joe'd been dumbfounded that Beth had actually started divorce proceedings, he'd told Ms. Schmidt that Beth could have anything she wanted for herself and the kids.

Anything she wanted, Beth thought bitterly. If he'd said that while they were together, this day would never have come. Well, the sooner she faced the ordeal, the sooner it would be over.

A knock sounded on the bedroom door, followed quickly by the appearance of Kate bearing a tray with a cup of coffee and two pieces of slightly burnt toast.

"What a surprise, sweetie," Beth said brightly, brushing away her tears and assuming a smile. One thing she and Joe had done right, she thought with a certain grim defiance, was to be good parents to their three children. Kate set the tray down on the antique washstand that doubled as a bedside table and flicked back her thick braids. She was gentle and thoughtful and had the potential to become a great beauty. Since the separation, she'd been striving hard to be mature, yet at times the whimsy of childhood flashed touchingly, making her vulnerable and precious.

"I made you breakfast, Mommy," Kate said, indicating the tray. "To cheer you up. But I think I pushed the dial on the toaster too far toward DARK."

Beth drew her daughter into her arms.

"Ah, Katie, aren't you mad at me? Josh and Cindy are."

"They're babies. They never notice the way Daddy's been acting toward you. I sure never thought you'd get divorced, though."

Beth hadn't thought so either. Secretly, she'd expected that once she'd started proceedings, Joe would wake up to a realization of what he'd been doing to her. Surely he'd understand she'd been driven to desperation by his unreasonable attitude. But she'd misjudged him. He wasn't the man she thought he was, the perfect storybook lover, husband, and father. She'd never looked at another man. Never wanted to. If Joe Columbine loved a woman, she had it all, she'd thought. What a cruel joke. He hadn't cared enough for her to make the smallest concession. He didn't know the meaning of growing and accommodating in a marriage.

But she was determined to do everything in her power to keep the children from suffering any more than they had to. Even in their small town, divorce was no longer a stigma. Children weren't ostracized by their schoolmates, many of whose own parents were divorced, some more than once. She'd read everything she could find on the effects of divorce on children, and the consensus of the experts seemed to be that the ones who adjusted best weren't turned against the other parent. She'd even managed to talk to Joe about it when he'd come to take the kids to dinner one night. They'd agreed that they wouldn't let their own resentments influence the children. She encouraged them to be with their father at every opportunity. Indeed, she thought, he was seeing more of them now than he had during this past year, when he'd joined every club in town to avoid being with her.

Kate had seen and understood. Nevertheless, Beth didn't want her to blame Joe.

"He's right in his own mind, honey," Beth said, sipping the too-strong coffee. "I guess Daddy just isn't ready for women's liberation. And you've heard him complaining about Mr. Springfield, his boss. Life isn't easy for him."

"I wish he'd just quit his job instead of taking it out on you, Mommy," Kate said simplistically.

"Jobs aren't that easy to come by, Kate. You can't just quit when things get hard." Beth winced inwardly. Wasn't she quitting on her marriage?

"But Daddy shouldn't take it out on you," Katie insisted. "Anyhow, he didn't start being mean to you until you got the job. Mr. Springfield was just as bad before you started to work, and Daddy never acted that way with you then."

"He feels my working means I don't think he can support us adequately," Beth said. "He was brought up to think that way, I guess. I'm sure he doesn't see himself as mean."

"Mom, you still love him," Kate said, watching her mother carefully. "*I* wouldn't love a man who called me a dope and said I neglected my kids."

"You heard, huh?" Beth said, smiling ruefully. "But I know you, Katie. You'd love him all the same, just as I do."

16

Kate's facade of maturity seemed to collapse all at once. "Then why are you getting a divorced?" she cried. "What's going to happen to all of us?"

Beth put down her coffee cup and drew the child back into her arms.

"It'll be okay, honey," she said comfortingly. "We'll really work on it so it'll be okay. Dad will be living right here in Bellemonte. It will be different, but we'll try to keep it from changing too much. At least now all the fighting will stop."

Just then, Josh and Cindy came clattering through the study into the room, Daisy waddling awkwardly behind them.

"Yeah, but the camping and the fun and stuff will stop, too," Josh said mournfully. He stared belligerently up at his mother.

Beth sighed. She never could look at her son without seeing Joe. It wasn't only that the boy was the spit and image of his father, from his slender hands and form to his brooding good looks. Even the sudden, frequent, and still somehow unexpected smiles that lit the dark Mediterranean faces were identical. But it was the worshipful way Josh unconsciously mirrored his father's thoughts and mannerisms that tore her troubled heart.

"Joshua Columbine, you all went camping with Daddy last weekend," Beth countered.

"It wasn't any fun without you. Daddy kept yelling at us to stop fighting, and he burned the hot dogs, and it rained."

"Honey, he always yells when you fight, he always burns the hot dogs, and he couldn't help that it rained," she said reasonably. But the unbidden picture of Joe earnestly "having fun" with the kids in her absence caught her unawares and made it almost impossible to answer Josh's complaining with just the right light touch. She could almost see Joe's dark hair falling across his forehead, his ratty old Woolrich jacket getting even more burn holes from the campfire as he tried to cook and pay

17

attention to the kids at the same time.

"It was different," Josh maintained stubbornly, the stubbornness, too, reminding her of Joe. He climbed up and sat cross-legged on the bed, regarding her solemnly as if expecting her to set things right in an instant. "It wasn't fun."

Daisy lifted her front paws as if to follow Josh onto the bed; then, as if thinking better of it considering her bulk, she sighed and stretched out with her head on Beth's bare foot.

Beth sighed, too. "It'll take some getting used to, kids. We're going to have to work at it."

Cindy stirred sloppily at a glass of instant orange juice, shuffling her feet in her father's big bedroom slippers, which she'd taken to wearing. Her pink nylon nightgown was smeared in places with blackberry jelly, and her dark ringlets fell over her eyes in disarray.

"I'm not going to work at it," she said. "I don't want a divorce." Snippiness was getting to be a way of life with Cindy.

"Cindy, *you* aren't getting a divorce," Beth said patiently. "I've explained to you that it isn't your fault, and you're not expected to take sides either. Daddy and I have been unhappy for long time now. You don't want that, do you?"

The little jaw set stubbornly. "You should just knock it off. That's what you tell Josh and me when we fight. Josh makes *me* unhappy, but I'm not divorcing him."

"Honey, it's not the same. *All* brothers and sisters fight. Parents aren't supposed to."

"Janie's parents fight. He blacked her eye."

"Do you want us to live like that?" Beth asked, appalled that Cindy seemed to accept physical violence so readily.

"You wouldn't have to, Mommy," she explained patiently. "Daddy would never black your eye."

"But we were fighting all the time. It made you cry."

"I'll . . . I'll get used to it and not cry anymore, Mommy,"

Cindy said, her dark eyes watchful. "You and Daddy could fight if you wanted."

Beth was beginning to feel overwhelmed. The entire conversation felt unreal.

"We don't *want* to fight, darling," she said, trying to be patient. "It's just that grown-ups change sometimes." She thought bleakly of Joe's shouted "I don't know if I *do* love you." Husbands and wives grow away from each other. They want different things out of life. Then they can't agree; they can't get along together, and they make themselves and their children miserable. It's better to separate than to start hating each other."

"You told us it's a sin to hate anyone," Josh said belligerently. "You said you shouldn't even hate Hitler and guys like that. Remember? When I asked you about my catechism lesson ore loving your neighbor."

"That's right, Josh. But sometimes when you have to live with someone who . . . who hurts you and makes you miserable . . . like Daddy did me . . . and," she added hastily, remembering her determination not to force them to take sides, "like I was doing to him, it's hard not to come to hate."

"You said it's a sin," he insisted uncompromisingly.

"Then I guess you could just say Daddy and I are avoiding the occasions of sin," she snapped, finally losing her patience. "Look, guys, I can't help it, okay? I would if I could. You'll just have to take my word for that. You're not going to lose either of us, though. You'll understand better when you're older."

Josh slid off the bed, stalking, stiff-legged, toward the door.

"You'll understand when you're older, you'll understand when you're older," Cindy mimicked, trailing in Josh's wake. "You always say that."

"Get dressed, kids. We have to be in the judge's chambers at nine," Beth said, making the bed. She ducked her head so

19

they wouldn't see her eyes. But she knew Kate wasn't fooled. She'd seen the tears.

"I love you, Mommy," she whispered and followed her brother and sister from the room.

Across town, the obnoxious ring of a cheap alarm clock woke Joe Columbine. He groaned and clapped a hand down to silence it. As he had every morning of the six weeks since he'd been gone, he threw an arm out to his left to find Beth and draw her near.

Of course she wasn't there. You'd think he'd learn. His hand was black and blue from smacking it against the cheap metal nightstand instead of Beth's rounded shoulder.

Outside the hotel, a four-wheel-drive vehicle with a bad muffler roared across the bridge. In the room next to his, one of the elderly, permanent Bantry House residents with chronic bladder problems slammed his door on his fifth trip to the bathroom, which the entire wing shared. A headache, which had become as chronic as his neighbor's bathroom trips, began to throb in Joe's temples.

"Damned silly woman," he growled into the pillow, referring to Beth.

Why couldn't she just stay the same sweet woman she'd always been? Why had she let these women's libbers get to her? All at once, having her own way was the most important thing in the world to her. You could have knocked him over with a feather when she'd actually gone and enrolled in college, then gotten a job to pay the tuition. Women's lib. That's what had changed her, even if it did infuriate her when he said so. They all thought they were so damned smart. Now you even had to fill quotas of women when hiring. And just let some mean-natured boss like Springfield dump on women the way he routinely did on men. Just let him try! Women yelled discrimination

20

and even sexual harassment so loud, the building fell down. They didn't want *equal* rights; they wanted the deck stacked neatly in their favor.

Beth was out of her mind to want to join the work force. For Pete's sake, didn't she realize how dog-eat-dog the work world had become? She acted as if working were fun! She could! The mortgage, utilities, food, and clothing weren't coming out of *her* pay. All she had to do was pay the tuition — which was greatly reduced since she was a university employee — buy a few clothes she wouldn't otherwise have needed, and bank the rest. It was *her* money.

He rolled over on the narrow bed and stood up, his mouth tasting like the Bellemonte limestone plant. A nagging memory of himself calling his salary *his* money stubbornly refused to be banished. He had to admit, he wished he'd leveled with Beth about the tuition. To be sure, he hadn't wanted her going to work and school; he loved having her at home. But that wasn't the real reason he'd refused to pay the tuition. The fact was, they just couldn't afford it. But he could hardly admit a thing like that to Beth. He'd never give her any reason to suspect they weren't doing fine financially. But the fact was that rising interest rates and the sluggish state of the economy had caused sales to drop sharply. He was about the only one of Springfield's staff who was moving anything at all.

He'd considered suggesting they rent the third-floor apartment again to ease the strain, but he'd made such a big deal of them having their very own "guest quarters," and the kids loved watching television upstairs in what they called the tree house because it was surrounded with trees. . . . Now he wished with all his heart he *had* suggested it. The rent money would have gone toward getting Beth started with a couple of courses anyhow. He hadn't been fair or honest to pretend he thought she'd be neglecting the kids by going to school, but he'd never expected his mild-mannered wife to defy him as she had. He couldn't have been more shocked if their gentle beagle had suddenly attacked him.

Yet how could he tell her he wasn't the big-shot real estate tycoon she and the families had always considered him? It was his place to provide for the family's needs. He'd known the time was coming when Beth would want to start college, and he should have been able to pay for it. But Springfield arbitrarily kept any big commissions for himself by refusing to let the agents show the most lucrative properties — although they, and particularly Joe, did most of the listing and legwork. No, he couldn't tell his wife the truth, that he simply couldn't afford college tuition. It had been a severe blow to his pride that she'd promptly found work and the means to pay it herself.

She didn't need him anymore.

Thinking of her going off to the campus every day bothered him, too. She looked about eighteen. Every smart-ass Joe College on campus, not to mention the liberal-minded professors, would be after her. She was not only beautiful but cute and sexy, too. He was so proud of her. After all these years, he still blessed the day she'd agreed to marry him. His lovely young bride.

But she'd grown up. He no longer knew her. He wasn't the center of her world anymore.

He pulled open the dresser drawer and took out a pair of shorts and a T-shirt. They were all a uniform shade of gray since he'd thrown everything in together at the laundromat last week. There hadn't seemed much point in making a separate load for six pairs of dark socks and a pair of dungarees he'd bought to take the kids camping. He swore again. Good thing he always sent his shirts to the laundry, or Springfield would be complaining about his appearance at work.

She'd picked a hell of a time to throw him out.

And to slap him with divorce papers. Things couldn't have been worse at work. If there was only some way to get his hands on some capital, he'd start a firm of his own. But that would probably mean a cut in income. And with a big house and three children, there just wasn't any way to get out from under Springfield's tyrannical thumb.

He'd always been willing to take a good deal of punishment in his work, figuring, rather fatalistically, that everyone was in for a certain amount of grief in this life and, since heaven had blessed him above most in his wife and children, he couldn't complain about his job. Or so he'd believed until this college thing.

He pulled on his almost-new bathrobe and picked up his towel, the same shade of gray as his underclothes. At home, in his and Beth's suite — as she'd called the study, bedroom, and bathroom wing with its three closets — he'd never bothered with a robe or much else. The kids respected their privacy. He thought of Beth, sleeping alone in the double cherry bed, with a physical yearning. There was a tight pain across his chest and a lump in his throat.

No use. No use hankering for what was gone.

Today would be the end of it.

He'd give years of his life to go back to the way things had been before. He pictured Beth, smiling gently, her slender waist swelled with pregnancy, leaning over the table in the kitchen rolling pie dough. Her long hair would be caught up and tied with a red ribbon, not cut in the new, short, and wildly becoming way she'd adopted since she began working.

Even now she looked too young to be a wife and mother. Yet, incredibly, her youthful beauty had contained a touch of earth mother and temptress, too. She'd been companion, child, wife, nurturer, and lover to him. He'd expected her to be all things to him forever.

He was out of toothpaste and brushed his teeth with water. His eyes appeared puffy to him, yet he'd lost weight. When all this was over, he'd think of getting a more permanent place. A small apartment, maybe. He'd have to learn to cook. Maybe he'd get used to living alone. Maybe he'd even find someone new someday.

After Beth?

The words echoed inside his head in his own shocked voice. Even *looking* at someone besides Beth was unthinkable. He must be going crazy! He wanted to love. But the woman he loved didn't want him anymore.

She said she was sick and tired of his chauvinism. She had every right to be, he supposed. But he was an old-fashioned Italian man like his father. He believed that it was his place to provide for his family and her place to cook and clean and smile when he came home. She'd been happy, he could have sworn it. How had the two of them gotten off the bicycle built for two they'd always ridden and drifted off into two separate worlds? He'd never been confused in his life before. From childhood, he'd known what he wanted and had gone after it. The bitter truth was that he still wanted Beth, but there was no going after her anymore.

He shaved and showered, cutting himself and having to borrow a bandage from the old man across the hall. He dressed in the dark brown blazer and tweed slacks Beth had given him for Christmas, along with the salmon-colored shirt she'd always said he looked handsome in. He remembered how proud she'd been to have paid for the clothing with her own money, not having had to ask him for cash or a credit card to go Christmas shopping. She'd said he looked like the young and handsome answer to a woman's prayer in that outfit.

As he started up the hill to the ionic-columned courthouse, he thought bitterly that he hoped she'd realize there were plenty of women out there who'd smile kindly on the young and handsome answer to a woman's prayer.

Beth was already waiting outside the judge's chambers with the kids and her lawyer, a slim, attractive woman who was also involved with the local chapter of NOW. She'd probably convinced Beth that she'd wasted nine years living with a chauvinist, Joe thought angrily.

His attorney was their family lawyer, who'd handled the transfer of the real estate and advised Joe to pay the fine for the speeding ticket even though he had *not* been speeding the night he'd been arrested. He said it was crazy to chalk up a night in jail on your record for a principle. He was honest and capable, though, and the matter should be easily settled; both he and Beth wanted to be fair where the kids and money were concerned. He'd always wondered at guys who tried to weasle out of child-support payments. One of his friends had said he resented paying one dime for food that his ex-wife's boyfriend might be eating. *Beth with a boyfriend!* Joe's vision blurred at the very thought.

"Hi, kids," he said, including Beth in his welcoming smile.

She smiled in return. Civilized. They were going to have a civilized divorce.

Civilized was the last thing he'd ever imagined he'd be in this circumstance. He'd been so much in love with her, so consumed with her, that the very thought of the most casual separation had filled him with passion and anxiety. Yet here he sat, about to get a divorce, exchanging casual smiles with her.

But what else could they do? They both loved the children too much to make a war prize out of them.

Judge Willoughby entered and nodded solemnly before seating himself behind his desk and motioning for them all to file in and find seats.

"I never expected to see you two here," he said flatly.

Beth flushed, deeply embarrassed, and dabbed at her eyes. *Damn. Don't cry, Beth.* Joe flexed his hands. What a stupid thing for the judge to say. Did he think they'd suddenly looked at each other after nine years and said, "Hey, I hate to tell you this, but we're just going to have to hang it up?"

Beth swallowed hard and put her handkerchief in her jacket pocket. She threw a quick, baffled look at Joe. *I don't want to be here! Oh, Joe, let's go home! Oh, Joe, love me again.*

Joe was staring obdurantly at his hands, clasped between his knees. His handsome face wore the shut, angry look she'd come to know so well in the last few months. His bulling look.

She sighed and met the judge's gaze.

He was a middle-aged, sandy-haired, pleasant-faced man who looked as though he ought to be coaching football with a bunch of happy kids instead of listening to a divorce action in chambers. He was also a good friend to both of them. They'd entertained him at neighborhood picnics in their big backyard. He was regarding Beth politely, solemnly, expecting an explanation.

"Nothing's forever, Judge Willoughby," she said in a small voice. "Sometimes people change . . ."

"Call me John; I've known you both too long for such formality. Who's changed?"

Beth's lawyer cleared her threat and picked up a sheaf of papers, but the judge threw her a warning glance before focusing back on Beth.

"Joe's changed," she said. "I hardly recognize him as the man I married."

"*I've* changed?" Joe interjected. "Boy, is that a laugh. You're the one who's changed. You used to be a gentle, loving little angel, and I nearly killed myself to give you anything you wanted."

"Only if *you* wanted me to have it. You wouldn't give me college tuition," she snapped.

He opened his mouth to tell her he couldn't afford the college tuition but the words stopped in his throat. To admit that seemed like admitting he wasn't a real man. Besides, her pretty mouth had taken on a stubborn look, so new and unwelcome.

"Well, that didn't stop you," he said instead. "You just went out and earned the tuition money yourself. You're saying you don't need me to take care of you as you did when we married. You aren't satisfied with what I can give you."

"Oh, Joe, you always start that, and it's not so. You always put me on the defensive. You want to own me, body and soul. You can't see that my being with you because I *want* to instead of because I *have* to is better."

"Better? *I* don't see that it's better. I say I made a bargain for a certain kind of wife, and you've reneged."

Beth shook her head in exasperation. "There's no use trying to talk to you, no use at all." She clamped her lips shut.

Beth's lawyer cleared her throat again and examined a well-manicured nail as she tossed back a shiny mane of chestnut hair. Joe's lawyer stared at them thoughtfully. He exchanged a look with the judge as Ms. Schmidt leaned forward.

"I really don't see that any of this is serving any useful purpose, Judge Willoughby," she said in a cultivated manner. "The marriage is obviously damaged irrevocably; we'd best get on with the means and terms of dissolution. Both parties are willing —"

"I'm not at all convinced of that," the judge interrupted, staring thoughtfully at Beth and Joe. His gaze drifted to the three children, who were huddled silent and miserable midway between their parents, as if they were determined not to show partiality.

27

"Look at these kids, you two," he said, anger creeping into his voice. "I directed you to bring them to this hearing on purpose. You're obviously superior parents; they're as bright and happy as any kids in this town. I would have sworn their home life was happy, too."

"That's just it, John," Beth cried in anguish. "It *was* happy. Now all we do is fight. We're hurting them, and we know it. I *have* to grow or I'll die. Joe doesn't . . . won't understand. We fight constantly. He's probably right; I'm not the woman he married. I grew up. The point is, we have no right to make our children live in a war zone. I *have* looked at them, and, to his credit, Joe has, too. We don't like what we've been doing to them."

"I'm glad you are cognizant of their position enough to have been thinking of that. But I'm not convinced divorce is the answer. Have you tried counseling?"

"Counseling!" Joe snorted. "That's the first thing everyone thinks of these days. That's what our parish priest said."

"He said he didn't know how to talk to you!" Beth put in sharply. "He said you were the most stubborn man he'd ever encountered and that maybe a secular counselor would do better than he could."

"Whatever. The point is, he thought I was a devil and you're an angel who can do no wrong. But we both know better than that, don't we, Beth?"

She flushed and shook her head angrily.

"I've known you both for years," the judge interjected. "I think you're both fine people. Intelligent people who ought to be able to deal constructively with the changes life brings your way. The fact is, I've seen too many cases where a marriage oughtn't to have been dissolved, and I was helpless to get through to the divorcing couple. I hope you'll show good enough sense to patch up your differences and work your way through your difficulties."

"I've seen some of those couples who 'patch up their differences,' " Beth said. "They work things out, all right. World War Three every day of their lives for forty years, but they don't divorce. They come to hate each other in the end. No, I'd rather we split while . . ." She faltered to a stop, not wanting to say what was in her heart: *while I still love him.*

Joe glanced at her sharply, but she stared down at her lap. He felt his face tighten into an expressionless mask.

"I agree with her, John," he said flatly. "I don't want to live in a marriage that's a battleground. We don't think it's good for the kids. No matter what happens, we're determined they're not going to suffer or have to choose between us."

He thought of the article Beth had cut out and sent to him about how children often got the notion that it was *their* fault their parents had separated. That if they'd been "better" kids, it wouldn't have happened. She'd scrawled a note on the margin urging him to keep assuring them, as she'd been, that it wasn't their fault, that they both still loved the children with all their heart. She'd always been a loving and intuitive mother. The thought that the children might blame themselves hadn't occurred to him. He remembered how they had always clustered around him and Beth when he came home from work each day, putting their little arms around their legs. Then he and Beth would kneel together and draw the children into their arms, so that the entire family was locked in a tight embrace. He shook his head to drive away the memory.

"The money or custody is no problem, your honor," Joe's attorney was saying. "Joe's currently living at the Bantry House, but when things settle down he'll get an apartment with room for the kids."

"Are you planning to keep the house on Elm Street?" the judge asked Beth.

She swallowed hard.

"We don't think we can afford to, your honor," she said, addressing him more formally, as Joe's attorney had done, now that he seemed to be accepting the notion of their splitting up. "The mortgage payment is no more than apartment rentals and upkeep, but the cost of heating such a house is high. I don't want Joe to live in a dump somewhere so I can stay in the house."

For the first time, sounds of dismay escaped the otherwise silent children. Everyone looked at them. Cindy was sobbing, trying to silence herself while Josh stared at her furiously, his own dark eyes wet. Kate cast her gaze on the floor and drew a hand up to shield her eyes from scrutiny.

Beth and Joe exchanged a pained glance.

This can't be happening, Beth thought.

The judge stared hard at the children. "Isn't it possible to keep the house?" he asked. "I think your kids have enough to deal with, having their parents' marriage breaking up, without losing their home and neighborhood friends, too."

Beth shook her head, not meeting his eyes. How could she explain that every day spent in the house that had once sheltered their love was deeply painful to her?

"Listen," Judge Willoughby continued, "there's been a great deal written recently about a divorce case out in Michigan. The judge directed that the couple couldn't sell the family home until the youngest child was eighteen. That'd be at least ten years, wouldn't it? How old are you, Cindy?"

"I'm six," she said tearily. She started toward her father uncertainly, then, glancing at her mother, stopped.

Beth's eyes filled at the mute evidence of Cindy's torn emotions.

"Go ahead, honey," she whispered. "Go hug your father."

The little girl ran to her father and climbed into his lap,

burying her face in his brown jacket. Joe's arms went around her tenderly; the love in his eyes seemed to embrace Beth, too.

Judge Willoughby cleared his throat awkwardly. "Hm, yes," he said. "Anyhow, this Michigan judge put the house in the *children's* custody. He gave the parents joint custody of their children. One would stay with them in the family house for a month, then move out to his own parents' home, and the other would move in. They alternated, month by month, as guardians in the family house. I saw it all on television. Everyone was as happy with the arrangement as it's possible to be."

Beth and Joe looked at each other.

"What would you think of a similar arrangement?" the judge asked.

"It would be fine, your honor," Joe said slowly, "except that neither of our parents lives here. But perhaps we might get an apartment . . . nothing special . . . which the one who wasn't enjoying custody at the moment might use."

Beth was staring tenderly at their children. Unbelieving hope was dawning in the three pairs of dark eyes. If it could only work! She looked at Joe, grateful that he'd agreed to consider it.

"I'm not sure we can afford to keep another apartment your honor," she said slowly. "I've been so worried that Joe isn't eating right while he's been staying at the Bantry House. He . . . he's not much of a cook, and restaurant meals are expensive."

Judge Willoughby's eyes glinted behind his horn-rimmed glasses. Abruptly he motioned the two lawyers to approach his desk.

"Would you folks — children, too — be good enough to step outside in the corridor for a moment?"

The Columbines filed out, Joe holding the door politely for his wife.

31

They stood awkwardly in the hallway. Joe asked the children how school was, then asked Beth if she'd like a cup of coffee.

"They might want us before you could return with it," she said with a wan smile to soften her refusal.

He nodded. They waited, listening to the rise and fall of voices within the judge's chambers.

"Beth, I don't mind staying at the Bantry House during my off month," he said suddenly. "I'd like being back home with the kids part of the time. But it's no place for you. Don't worry. Maybe I can get a part-time job to pay for a better place."

She shook her head. "You work too hard now, Joe. Look, I don't have to go to school as I'd planned when the new term starts. I'll use the tuition money on the mortgage payment so we can rent an apartment."

"But you want to go to college. That's what all this fuss is about."

"I guess it's all up to the judge anyhow, isn't it?" she said.

Joe's attorney, smiling broadly, opened the door and motioned them back in. The children, pale but excited, stood along the front of the desk.

"Mr. and Mrs. Columbine, I've decided to grant your request for a divorce," Judge Willoughby said solemnly. "With the provision we discussed that you may not sell the house until Cindy is eighteen. And provided you'll agree to a trial separation. I make no bones about being convinced a divorce would be a grave mistake in this case. However, you do have an ideal situation in which to share custody of your children. Joe, at the last neighborhood picnic you mentioned that your third-floor apartment is empty and that you and Beth had no plans to seek a new tenant. I am hereby directing that you move into it." He smiled widely, obviously pleased with his decision.

The children started cheering wildly. Joe and Beth exchanged dazed glances.

I can't live under the very same roof with him, she thought, panic-stricken. How will I ever be able to keep my hands off him?

Joe's face was taking on a look of incredulity, like a condemned man who'd been given a stay of execution. He stared at his family, his face contorted with emotion. Suddenly everything seemed all right. But how could he keep away from Beth?

"You're not going to grant the divorce?" Beth faltered. "I thought Pennsylvania had no-fault divorce, and if the two parties agreed . . ."

"I am allowed considerable discretion in such matters, Beth. I am not convinced an immediate divorce is in the best interest of either you and Joe or your children. If, in nine months, one month for each year of your marriage, you both still want it, I'll grant it with no necessity for all that nonsense of proving blame. My function is to be as concerned for your children's welfare as you both seem to be. I admit, I am taking considerable license in denying you an immediate divorce. But I know you both, and I am certain that neither of you has a compelling reason for wanting to be free, such as a third person waiting —"

"Good Lord, no, what do you take us for?" Joe cried.

Judge Willoughby couldn't hide his smile. "Exactly. Therefore, I'm granting a legal separation. Beth and the children will occupy the first two floors of the family house, and Joe the third-floor apartment. You will share custody of your children under conditions and schedules you will agree upon."

"It seems a reasonable solution," Beth said slowly. She glanced at her husband. "Do you think it can work, Joe?"

His heart was beating painfully. *Yes,* he thought, *if I can keep from beating down your bedroom door and loving you.* He forced his face into a decorous expression. For a split second he thought he saw the same naked longing in Beth's eyes that he was forcing himself to hide. But he had to stop thinking of that now. The important thing was that he'd been banished, and now he was being welcomed home.

For to Joe, home would always be where Beth and his children were.

"We'll make it work, Beth," he said quietly. "I promise."

2

They filed out of the judge's chambers, the children chattering elatedly and the parents stunned into silence. They went down the courthouse steps together, past the lovely old Ionic columns and the decorative fountain, and stopped on the sidewalk in front of the war memorial. Joe gazed at his family with ill-concealed delight.

"Do you think John wanted the kids present in order to manipulate us?" he asked, smiling irrepressibly at Beth. "I mean, he as much as admitted he's really stretching things to require a trial separation."

"I wouldn't put it past him," she replied.

Their respective lawyers emerged, talking in quiet voices. Joe watched Ms. Schmidt's pretty wine-colored dress whip about in the May wind.

"Do you think we can make this arrangement work, Beth?" he said.

Don't look at him, Beth told herself. She knew exactly how he'd appear to her — big, handsome, incredibly appealing. His eyes would be black and soft. The expression in them would make her knees feel like putty. She'd have to remind herself not to lift her arms for his embrace, right here on Allegheny Street. *Of course we can't make it work, you dope!* she felt like shouting. How could they possibly manage to live together . . . yet not really together . . . when their physical desire for each other was as fresh as it had been when they'd first married?

Yet for the children's sake they *had* to make it work. She

was still bemused by Judge Willoughby's solution to the problem. For Joe to move into the third-floor apartment would pose no financial drain at all. And he would actually be on the premises with his children, where they could see each other at will. Separating him from the kids had been her biggest worry all along. Joe and his children belonged to a mutual adoration society. No matter how badly matters had deteriorated between her and her husband, she could never, never fault him for his parenting of their children.

Even his refusal to stay home and take care of them on the nights she had classes had been directed against her, not them; she recognized it as a ploy to force her to stay home, although it hadn't worked.

"We'll have to do our best, Joe," she said softly. "It's a solution. If we hadn't been so bent out of shape over . . . over being separated, we'd have surely thought of it ourselves."

"I suppose so." His tone sounded doubtful, but when she glanced at him, he was looking at the children with shining eyes.

"Oh, Daddy, I'm so glad, glad, glad you're coming home," Cindy cried ecstatically, jumping up and down. Even solemn Kate put her arms around his waist and smiled.

"You'll be there when Daisy has her puppies, Dad," Josh said, grinning.

Joe turned to Beth at this reminder of Daisy's condition. "Did you take her to the vet? Does he have any idea when to expect them?"

Beth's mouth tightened imperceptibly, but she refrained from saying that taking *his* dog to the vet was really his responsibility. She nodded shortly.

"He saw her yesterday. He had a fit when he saw she's pregnant, since she's scarcely a full-grown dog herself. He said he can't be specific about when to expect the pups, that *we*

36

should have seen signs of estrus and confined her. But from the size of her, he supposes it will be soon."

"I'm sorry, Beth," Joe said unexpectedly. "You told me to get her taken care of. I promise I'll see to it as soon as the pups are weaned. But we shouldn't have too much trouble getting homes for half-hound puppies in a county full of hunters like this."

"Finding homes for them, Daddy?" Cindy cried. "We can't find homes for Daisy's pups. They're ours."

Joe shook his head firmly. "No, sweetheart, your mother didn't even want *one* dog; we can't stick her with a whole litter of them. We'll find good homes for them."

Beth fidgeted with her purse. This was ludicrous. They'd just come from getting legally separated, and here they stood on Allegheny Street, discussing Daisy's unborn pups.

"When . . . when are you going to move in upstairs?" she asked shyly.

"This evening after work, if that's okay with you. I'd better get back to work now. Springfield's none too happy that I took off this morning."

"We'll come help you, Dad," Josh said with the exaggerated casualness of the big, cool guys in the neighborhood. "We'll meet you at the Bantry House at five."

Joe's eyes locked on Beth's intimately, although his expression remained detached and polite. She felt as if he'd caressed her. "Is that okay with you, Beth?"

She nodded silently, trying hard not to smile. He was really coming home.

"We'll just eat at a take-out hamburger place, if you don't mind," he said. "I'll go to the mall for some utensils we don't have upstairs and to buy some groceries."

"Yes, that's all right."

Joe hugged the kids, nodded to her, and strode off down

Maple Street to his office, feeling a great deal happier than when he'd entered the courthouse. He couldn't stop smiling. Indeed, he smiled all the way down the street to Springfield Realty. His employer was watching from his private office when Joe entered the front door.

"Back here, Columbine," the spare Mr. Springfield called peremptorily.

Joe nodded to the other employees in the communal outer office and went into Mr. Springfield's private suite, shutting the door behind him.

"Leave it open, Columbine," his employer said. "Don't suppose there's anyone out there who doesn't know you and your missus had a divorce hearing this morning." Joe stiffened and moved toward the desk, not obeying Mr. Springfield.

"I'm sure they can hear all you're saying whether it's open or not, sir," he said through clenched teeth.

For a moment he thought Springfield would force the issue of his deliberate insubordination, but the older man apparently thought better of it and leaned back, lighting his cigar. Joe stared at him expressionlessly. Even after all the years he'd endured his boss's insults and meddling into his private life, it was difficult to believe Springfield could be so callous and crude. He'd inherited the firm his grandfather had started and enjoyed all the advantages of wealth and a good education. But he was as uncouth as any penniless, barefoot boy out of the hills, and he might have spent his years at college sweeping floors for all the polish or discernment he had acquired. Springfield acted as though having money eliminated the need for basic human courtesy and kindness.

"Well, did you and your missus call it quits?" Springfield asked bluntly.

Joe tightened his jaw in fury. With all his heart he longed to tell his employer it was none of his damned business, but he realized only too well how high the unemployment figures were. He loved the real estate business, he loved helping people find just the right property for their needs, and there was very little about it he didn't know. For the thousandth time, he wished Springfield would retire and let him and the other employees do their work without constantly criticizing and interfering.

There was a slight rustle from a chair on the other side of the room, and for the first time Joe noticed that Mandy Ferguson, Springfield's secretary, was sitting there, looking somewhat embarrassed. She was a big flamboyant woman of about thirty, a crackerjack who, everyone knew, was looking for a man.

"I'll come back later to get the rest of your dictation, Mr. Springfield," she said with a sympathetic glance at Joe.

"Sit down," Springfield snapped. "Might as well stay put; this won't take long. Well, Columbine, are you really divorcing?"

Joe drew a long, steadying breath.

"Not at present Mr. Springfield," he said quietly. "We're separating legally, but I'm going to be living in our third-floor apartment."

Springfield stared at him balefully while Mandy fidgeted. Finally he snorted derisively.

"Damned modern nonsense," he snapped. "Well, just see it doesn't interfere with your work, you hear?"

"Yes, Mr. Springfield. Is there anything else?"

The older man waved his hand in dismissal. Joe turned politely and started to leave the office. As he reached his desk, Springfield's intimidating voice arrested him.

"By the way, Columbine, we've sold that piece of mountain land you showed last week. Information's on your desk. See you take care of ordering the title search."

Joe nodded and reached for the folder that Mandy had

placed in the center of his desk.

We sold it, did we? he thought grimly. But like most of the sales in Springfield Realty, it was Joe who had shown it.

When Joe arrived at the Bantry House after work, his children were already waiting for him in the lobby. They clattered up the stairs at his heels as he tugged his necktie loose and undid the top button of his shirt. He unlocked the door to his room and, before he'd even zipped shut his toiletry case, the kids had opened the rickety bureau and wardrobe and were pulling out his belongings and piling them every which way into two suitcases.

"C'mon, Dad, that's everything, isn't it?" Josh said, as if anxious to see the last of his father's room at the Bantry House.

"You forgot my slippers under the bed," he said, amused and touched.

"Oh, Daddy, you bought a new pair," Cindy said reproachfully. "Your old ones are home, under my bed. They're perfectly good."

"These are only cheapos, honey. We can leave them," Joe said gently. He stroked his daughter's hair. "It's going to be great seeing you guys all the time again."

Kate leaned against his arm, frowning slightly. "Why don't you come *all* the way home, Daddy?" she asked softly. "Can't we forget about this separation? You haven't stopped loving Mommy, have you?"

Joe sat down slowly and put his arm around Kate. A muscle in his jaw worked convulsively.

"Katie, I know this is going to be hard for you to understand," he said, "especially since your mother and I always led you to believe that love makes the world go around. I guess we believed it ourselves. Now, it really isn't important whether I love your mother or not; the fact is, we just don't see eye to

40

eye on things anymore."

"Dad, I think that's a bunch of junk," Josh said spiritedly. "Mommy said the same thing this morning, only her words were just a little bit different. You're always hollering at us to respect each other's viewpoints and opinions. How come you and Mom aren't doing it?"

Joe stared at his son, at a loss for words. Nevertheless, he tried valiantly to explain. "It's *because* we're trying to respect each other that we've separated," he said. "Mom thinks one way; I think another. We're two people with what they call 'irreconcilable differences.' "

"Baloney, Daddy!" Josh stared up at his father, reminding Joe of himself at that age. Not that he'd have dared sass his father like that.

"Now, look, son —"

"We were so *happy*, Daddy." Kate, always the peacemaker, leaned her head against his. "I guess we didn't appreciate it until it was gone. That's all Josh is trying to say. He doesn't mean to be fresh."

"I know, honey," Joe said huskily.

"Wouldn't you like being Mommy's husband again?" Cindy asked wistfully. She was kneeling next to him on the bed. In a gesture that was poignantly reminiscent of Beth, she buttoned his shirt and drew the knot of his tie neatly into place.

"Now, Cindy, if we're going to make this thing work, you guys will have to forget about trying to get your mother and me back together," he said unsteadily. "You can't make Christmas come just by wishing it."

Kate sighed deeply. Josh grinned. "At least you just admitted it would be like Christmas being back with Mom."

"Now, Joshua Columbine, I did no such thing," Joe protested.

But Josh wasn't listening. He'd picked up the smaller suitcase and was running down the hall with it.

Beth had eaten a solitary supper of leftover manicotti.

She was painfully aware of the ache she was feeling. It was tough being left out, even though there would have been no graceful way to be included in Joe's homecoming. When she heard his car pulling into the driveway at the rear of the house and his key in the lock of the cellar door, she retreated to her own bedroom, tactfully leaving Joe with the children to enjoy his first night back under the family roof. She heard them happily hauling his groceries and clothing through the cellar door and up the tower stairs all the way to the third floor. At last they came back downstairs and, one by one, came into her room to say good night. Their eyes were shining, and they all seemed more relaxed than they'd been in weeks. She kissed them and sent them off to their baths and beds.

Falling asleep wasn't easy for her that night, knowing Joe was preparing for bed in the room directly above hers. She thought of his broad shoulders and slender form. He'd be bathing in the tiny turn-of-the-century tub nestled under the eaves in the third-floor bathroom, trying to rinse the suds away with the rubber hose attachment. She hoped he didn't whack his head when he got out of the tub. How she wished he were coming to her bed! She gulped as she pictured his dark, curly head on the pillow beside hers. That sort of thinking would get her nowhere, she admonished herself sternly. When they'd applied for the divorce, they'd effectively turned their backs on all that. She set her jaw in determination. It wouldn't be easy, doing without Joe's presence in her life . . . and in her heart. She'd never denied that she loved him. She needed him, too, although not in the superficial way that seemed so important to him. Now that she was managing her own life and earning a salary, he said she didn't need him anymore.

Oh, Joe, she thought, I need you to *love*. Why isn't that enough?

She finally fell asleep.

Something woke her. She lay still, confused for a moment, listening. There was a faint fluttering above her in the big room. Her heart lurched. She knew that sound only too well. Once before, a bat had flown into the house when the cellar door had been left open. Tonight Joe and the children had been carrying his belongings in that way; it must have happened again.

Nothing in the entire world terrified Beth as much as bats. The flesh all over her body seemed to crawl as she realized she was sharing her bedroom with one. She pulled the sheet over her head in an instinctive withdrawal from terror — and screamed.

The sound was primitive and penetrating.

Joe, lying awake and yearning for Beth in the room upstairs, heard it and shot bolt upright. He hit the floor running and didn't stop until he'd switched on the study light outside Beth's bedroom door.

"What's wrong? Beth, what's wrong?" He blinked in the sudden light. Then, seeing the circling bat through her open door, he slammed it shut, confining the bat with the screaming, quivering mound under the sheet.

"Hang on, Beth, I'll be back with the tennis rackets," he shouted, racing for the hall closet. The last time a bat had gotten in, he'd captured it neatly between two rackets and released it outside.

"What is it, Daddy?" The kids were standing sleepily in their doorways, watching him.

"Go back to bed, kids, it's just a bat," he said reassuringly. "I'll take care of it."

They blanched and slammed their doors. Joe grinned as he heard three little bodies plop into three beds. No doubt they'd all pulled the sheets over their heads, too.

He took the tennis rackets from the closet and ran back to the bedroom, darting inside, then slamming the door shut so the bat couldn't escape to another part of the house. Beth was still cowering under the covers; he could see the shape of her heaving shoulders in the dim light.

"Hang on, honey, I'll get it," he said, switching on the bedside lamp. Beth peeped out from under the sheet, lowering it just enough to watch the circling bat in fascinated horror.

Joe took a couple of swats at it but couldn't reach it in the high-ceilinged room. "Don't worry, honey, I'll get it," he said, clambering up onto the bed. He loomed over Beth, and, despite her terror, he thought his presence seemed to reassure her a little. He watched carefully as the bat careened around the room, gauging the time he could hit it. When it passed over the bed again, his lightning shot, swift and delicate so as not to kill the frightened creature, dashed it against the wall above the bed. It plummeted swiftly, landing directly on Beth.

She shot up from the bed, tearing the sheet away from her. The confused bat fluttered across her neck and breasts. She screamed again and again, her body shuddering violently, but her arms frozen to such rigidity that she couldn't brush it away.

"Oh, get it off me, Joe! Oh, the filthy, filthy thing!"

He jumped down beside her and deftly flicked the bat away from her, then pounced on it with the two rackets, capturing it neatly between them.

"I've got it, Beth, I've got it. Come on, now, can you open the window screen for me so I can put it outside?"

Beth was nearly convulsed with fear and revulsion, but she nodded bravely, unable to take her eyes from the ugly animal, whose teeth were bared by the pressure of the racket. She staggered to the window and struggled with the levers at the bottom of the screen, lifting it until Joe could lean out and launch the bat into the night. He dropped the rackets to the ground, slammed the screen into place, and turned to hold Beth, who was shuddering uncontrollably and shaking her head as she gazed down at her lace-trimmed white cotton nightgown and slender arms.

"The awful, awful thing. I was afraid he'd bite me. He felt so dirty, so creepy." She began trembling as if she'd been standing in ice water, and her face was so alarmingly white that Joe was afraid she'd faint. She seemed close to hysteria. Without a word, he swept her into his arms and carried her into the adjoining bathroom. She was shuddering so strongly that Joe had trouble holding her, despite her mere one hundred pounds.

He pushed the glass shower door back as far as it would go, then lowered her gently into the bathtub and turned on the taps full force. He pulled Beth forward, stripping the gown off over her head and throwing it toward the hamper, then reached for a cake of English lavender soap, a birthday gift from him the year before. He lathered it between his hands, determinedly squelching the thought that he hadn't given her anything for her birthday this year, to demonstrate his displeasure with her. The thought shamed him. He pushed her gently back into the water.

"See, darling, it's all right. I've thrown the nightgown in the laundry hamper and I'm washing your arms and neck where the bat touched you," he said soothingly. "Relax, sweetheart, just let the water wash you. It's all right now. Does that feel better?" He lathered her rapidly, gently washing her face, her neck, shoulders, and breasts. She seemed only half-conscious of what he was doing. Her eyes were wide, the pupils dilated, and her face and body were as pale as alabaster. He was acutely, piercingly aware of her soft beauty. Oh, God, what had he gotten himself into?

Beth moved sensuously in Joe's arms. It felt so good to have him touching her. His hands were caressing her gently, soothing and comforting her. She drifted languidly on a cloud of well-being, feeling protected, cherished.

Gradually other emotions stirred to life. Desires she'd long denied were pulsing within her, rising in intensity, clamoring to be assuaged. *This was unreal!* Here they were, separated according to the laws of the sovereign state of Pennsylvania, and he was performing this most intimate service for her. Her every nerve ending tensed as her longing grew. Still he kept lathering, gently splashing warm water over her. He murmured reassuring words. He was so handsome, so virile! She wanted him so much.

Her gaze wandered over his broad, muscular chest. She ached to reach out and touch the soft mat of hair, to trace it down to where it disappeared into his pajama bottoms, riding low on his hips. She sighed softly, and her trembling ceased. Her body was electrically responsive to his touch.

He ought to stop, Joe told himself sternly. They were separated, for heaven's sake. But Beth's smooth body felt so good beneath his hands. Her big eyes looked on his. He could see that the fire threatening to engulf him was growing in her, too.

"Joe, you're so . . . thank you, Joe, I was so frightened. Oh, Joe, if you hadn't been here . . ."

She reached up languorously and enclosed his face with her wet hands. Joe's body clamored dangerously at her touch. "You're so beautiful, Valentine," he cried, leaning toward her. Their lips met as he teetered above her. The kiss was soapy, teary, and very sweet. Automatically Joe reached down to enfold his wife, forgetting his precarious balance over the tub. Suddenly he plunged into the full bathtub on top of Beth.

They were both submerged for a moment and came up gasping as water flooded over the edge onto the bathroom floor. Beth sputtered in surprise, then started to laugh in delight. She

46

clung to Joe, convulsed.

"Turn off the water and open the drain, or we'll drown," she choked out between paroxysms of laughter.

Joe struggled clumsily erect and complied. The water level started to drop. He was clad only in pajama bottoms, which clung wetly and showed Beth just how much in need of her he truly was. He had as much soap on him as she did. He pulled the glass door shut and drew her up beside him, turning on the shower to wash away the soapsuds. They stood, embracing as the cool water poured over them, their desire growing quickly. At last Joe turned off the water and dropped his pajama bottoms, stepping neatly out of them. He reached for a towel and began blotting the water from Beth, kissing her as he went. Her skin seemed to glow from the heat of each kiss. She was moaning softly and laughing, too, and as Joe climbed out of the tub, holding her hand to help her, she hurried back into his arms. He picked her up again, this time carrying her to the bed and laying her down gently, pulling the tumbled bedding to the bottom. Then he stretched out beside her, kissing her lips as he did so.

They clung together, their hands caressing gently but with a growing urgency as they inhaled the fragrance of their damp hair and skin.

"How could we ever think we could stay apart?" Joe whispered huskily. "Oh, Beth, I've missed you so much."

"And I've missed you, darling." Her eyes were swimming with happy tears, and she reached forward, nibbling on his earlobe. The result was electrifying. Joe twined his hands in her short, curly hair and drew her back gently to kiss her throat and shoulders.

"Oh, damn, Beth, you're the most beautiful, exciting woman . . ." He felt as though he were surrounded by a vibrating, fragrant aura of sensual emotion. He wanted her body desperately, but yearned even more to bring her sweet spirit close again. She turned toward him, and they were pressed lip to lip, breast to chest, and thigh to thigh, their arms tight around each other. He felt Beth's hot tears on his shoulder and smiled against her velvet lips. Beth always cried when she was deeply moved. She'd cried when she'd accepted his marriage proposal — though she'd been smiling, too. How could they, of all people, have gotten to the point of separating?

"Do you want me one-tenth as much as I do you, Valentine?" he murmured against her soft cheek.

"Oh, yes, Joe," came her smothered reply as her lips bestowed tiny, butterfly-light kisses all over his face and neck. "You're talking too much, sweetheart."

"You always said you liked the words of lovemaking."

"We've talked too much lately. There are other ways of saying I love you, I want you, I was made for you."

He drew back a little and smiled down at her. "You want me, then? You're willing to have me back?"

She smiled mistily. "How did we ever think we could stay apart?" she whispered. "We belong together."

He sighed happily. "Yes, love, we'll be together. Come to me, come to me . . ."

Happily, she did so. The sweet melding and explosion were as certain a consummation of their marriage as they had been the first time. They affirmed their reunion delightedly and without reservation, filling the room with their shared passion. At last, lip to lip, they slumbered.

Joe awakened to the gentle conversation of the mourning doves that lived in the eaves of the house, and to the blissful realization that Beth still lay cradled in his arms. Her face was against his chest, and her gentle breathing stirred the matted hair. He lay still, savoring the feel of her silken body against

48

his, the cool of the morning, and the sound of the doves' quiet cooing.

As if sensing his wakefulness, Beth stirred and murmured, reaching sleepily for his kiss. In moments she was fully awake and filled with passion, very gentle this time. Their swift, tender lovemaking was like a sweet postscript to the night.

Joe finally drew away to gaze tenderly at her. Her eyes were deep and dreamy, free of the terror that had started the wonderful magic between them.

"Beth, almost every man in this old world is searching for just what I have, a beautiful, passionate wife who's a good companion, a wonderful mother and homemaker . . . sweet, bright kids. I can't believe I was stupid enough to almost blow it all."

She smiled lovingly. "Is that an apology, Joe?"

He kissed the tip of her nose and toyed with a tendril of her hair. His eyes shifted from her eyes to her lips. He opened his mouth, but closed it in embarrassment.

Beth watched him, aware that he was having difficulty verbalizing his contrition. She smiled gently. "It isn't too hard, Joe," she urged fondly. "Just say, 'I'm sorry, Beth.' "

He put his head down on her breast and murmured, "I am sorry, honey."

Joy flowed through her, and she kissed the top of his head. She had thought her happy world was falling apart, and instead it was being restored to her. She pulled Joe's head up to kiss his lips. "I'm so happy," she cried softly. "Oh, Joe, I'm sorry, too, that it took such drastic measures to make you realize what you were doing to our marriage by your attitude."

"I've always been a hardhead, Beth," he said earnestly. "I promise I'll never yell at you and hurt your feelings again, and if you insist on going to school, well, then you have my permission."

Beth frowned, and a tiny warning flag seemed to go up in her mind.

"Just what are you apologizing for, Joe?" she asked slowly.

"For being selfish and spoiled. For not letting you do what you had your heart set on." He stopped and watched her warily, as if sensing that she wasn't reacting as he'd expected. He laughed uneasily and made a deprecating motion. "I'll do better, Beth. I'll be more permissive and understanding. After all, no man can have *everything* he wants; I'll just thank God that I've got most of what I want. I'll pay your tuition, honey. After all, you take such good care —"

"I take such good care of you. So you're giving me permission to go to school."

He nodded and began nuzzling her breast. "And no one could do it better," he said with tender suggestiveness.

Beth lay very still, melting love struggling with angry disappointment. She thought he'd been truly changing, but he was the same old Joe. He was giving her *permission* to go to school.

"Well, Joe," she said with an effort, "let's see you put your good intentions to work. I've got exactly thirty minutes to haul those kids out of bed, feed them, get them off to school, load the washing machine, and leave the house. Are you ready to help?"

"You mean you're going to work?" he cried incredulously. "After last night?"

"Of course." She pushed him firmly away so that he had to scramble to avoid landing on the floor. As she swung her legs over the side of the bed, she reached for her robe.

"Beth, *please!*" he said, facing her across the bed.

"Please what, Joe?"

"I said I'd pay the damned tuition if you just can't live without knowing the difference between all the damned King Henrys. But quit your job, honey. It's made you so different."

"It's made me different, all right," she said grimly. "It's made me realize I haven't been getting a fair shake in this marriage. I've accepted myself at *your* valuation for years, a sort of pretty numbskull who can bake a mean cheesecake and keep the kids clean and who's happy to be bedded at will. No, Joe, I'm afraid you did blow it. If you'd paid the tuition as you always led me to believe you would, this revolution might not have happened. But I think it's better that it did. Don't you see? You were only married to *part* of me, the part that lived for you and the kids. What about the part that's just *me?*"

"Here we go again," he said, forcing a laugh. "Beth has to 'find herself.' She's got to campaign for equal rights. Get the right to belly up to the bar with the guys."

"Don't be silly," she snapped, allowing her resentment at his derogatory manner to surface in spite of her determination to remain calm. "I just want to be treated like any other intelligent human being, respected for the work I do and not expected to be responsible for the entire running of *our* household and rearing of *our* children. I'm doing important work, do you realize that? Professor Ternan is writing a book on geophysics. He knows all there is to know about that, but he can't string two words together into a comprehensible sentence on paper. I'm *doing* that for him. He explains the principle of the subject to me, and I try to put it into understandable language. I read it back to him to be sure I haven't made a technical error. He says I'm the best secretary-editor he's ever had. And, working for him, I've found the incentive to start developing my own research and writing skills, too. Did you know that? No, you haven't been paying attention to anything I've been doing that doesn't concern Joe Columbine directly. I've got a novel partly outlined. Professor Ternan says it's hard to believe I've learned so much so fast."

"In other words, the marvelous, remarkable, brilliant Professor Ternan thinks you're just too wonderful for words," Joe retorted. "And you expect me to sit by smiling!"

"Oh, for heaven's sake, you haven't the slightest call to go making like a wild Italian husband," she said scornfully.

"That's what you say. What the hell do you know about men? I've been protecting you all these years."

"Well, since I'm twenty-nine years old, I really think you can stop now," she replied sweetly, opening her bureau drawer to take out underclothing and stockings. Joe stared at her desperately.

"Beth, I know you were as happy as I was that we'd gotten back together last night," he cried. "Now, damn it, either you quit that job or I march right back upstairs."

"Better start marching, Joe," she said quietly. "It's become a matter of principle now, and I can be stubborn, too, when it comes to principles."

"Beth Columbine, this is your last chance!"

She gave him a sad look. His hair lay tousled on his forehead, and his magnificent body . . . well!

"No, Joe, no ultimatums. You may not have my soul."

He turned abruptly, crossed to the tub in two strides, retrieved his soggy pajama bottoms, and wrung them out with an angry twisting motion. He pulled them on, wincing at the clamminess, and strode back into the bedroom.

"I won't be back," he said loftily from the doorway. His air of haughty dignity was marred by the wet pajamas flapping around his bare ankles. Beth couldn't stop herself. She chuckled audibly. Joe stalked indignantly through the study and up the stairs to his apartment.

Beth's laughter died. With a feeling of resignation she went about her morning chores.

3

After several false starts, the old station wagon coughed itself into motion. Joe had bought it several years ago so Beth could haul children and bring home garage-sale acquisitions. The fuel pump was going. Joe, who was a whiz at fixing automobiles, had promised to replace it months ago. She would have to take care of it before winter set in. She supposed she'd have to take it to a garage. Joe was procrastinating, she knew, because she was using the station wagon to go to work.

The thought made her frown. She'd spent little of the money she earned — just enough for tuition and gasoline and a few clothes. After all, she'd only started the job to pay her tuition, and she refused to fall into the trap of getting accustomed to a higher standard of living. She had taken pride in the increasing bank account and had dreamed vaguely of Joe someday being able to start his own business. But she'd prudently kept quiet about the amount she'd accumulated since Joe was so hostile about her work.

She was dressed simply in a gray blazer and plaid skirt, predominantly red but with white, black, and gray. She thought of the lovely cotton nightgown, trimmed with hand-crocheted lace, soaking in the basement laundry tray. She hoped she wouldn't think of the bat every time she wore it.

Or see Joe's tender face. Or feel his gentle hands on her body. Determinedly, she fought back a rush of passionate arousal and turned left on Spring Street. She waited at the school intersection as the traffic lady conducted children safely across. *Her* children were walking to school in Joe's company, as they'd done before he'd moved to the Bantry House. She knew it was a happy morning for them and was profoundly grateful that he was such a good father. The traffic lady smiled and motioned her on.

Why had it all blown up? They'd always been magically compatible lovers as well as darned good friends. True, Joe had always been protective of her, but she'd loved the attention. What woman wouldn't? Now she realized her seeming dependence on him was probably as much to blame for the rift as his stubbornness.

She *had* seemed to change overnight, she knew that. She'd expected Joe to assimilate the change as quickly as she had and to feel the same thrill of excitement she did at meeting new challenges. What a foolish, vain expectation! He wouldn't — couldn't — change. He would always see her success at this new endeavor as a rejection of his protective care. For months she'd tried to explain that it was nothing of the kind. But he insisted that the only way they could ever be together again "the way they used to be" was if Beth quit her job. His pride was hurt. If she loved him, she'd care how he felt.

Sauce for the goose, she thought grimly. If he loved me, he'd care how *I* feel!

But that line of reasoning had only reduced him to a sullen silence. Now she wanted to give in to him. With all her heart she wanted them to be together again.

But she knew instinctively that if she gave in — if she let him dictate how she might spend her own life — the relationship she salvaged would be irreparably damaged. And as surely as she breathed, she and Joe would have lost respect for each other.

Ironically, all the trouble stemmed from a job she'd never expected to have, a job that was only a means to an education.

But Joe's ultimatum that morning had made it infinitely more. It was a symbol now, but not of a power struggle — for she'd never willingly engage in anything so childish, nor had she ever tried to "win" Joe over. Now he was willing to pay her tuition, but she knew it was only a concession he was willing to make to get their lives back on his terms. He was acting like a weary parent, worn down by a child's whining for candy. If she accepted his offer to pay her tuition, he'd resent her as much as if he were a spineless parent and she a bullying child. No, although it was a temptation to give in and throw herself wholeheartedly into school and her own writing, such a course would only delay the day of reckoning. As she'd pointed out to Joe that morning, keeping her job was a matter of principle.

As she battled the traffic to the university, she thought wistfully of the days before their alienation. She'd been so busy. There'd been changing muddy clothes and popping warm cookies into little mouths. She would always remember that part of her life with melting love. Joe, too, had been in his glory in those days. He'd kissed her and the children reluctantly goodbye each morning and hurry home to them each evening. In the hours that intervened, each had worked hard and happily for the good of their family.

Although she always had lots of work to do in the big house, she'd still found time for herself. For years she'd been telling herself, "When the children are all in school . . . ," and she'd been ecstatic when that time had come. Until that morning she hadn't told Joe about the Arthurian novel she'd been outlining. She doubted very much if the information had registered with him even now. Her extensive reading and excellent memory had served her so far as she outlined the novel, but she needed much more data to write the book. The whole venture back into school, while glowing bright in her fantasies, had scared her, too. She'd done well by herself, she thought proudly, but

55

how she longed for Joe's support and encouragement.

Beth thought of their lovemaking the night before, and tears stung her eyes. *That* most definitely must not happen again, she admonished herself sternly, suppressing the thought of how his arms had felt, of his matted chest hair under her cheek when she'd awakened that morning. He'd been back under the family roof for less than five hours, and they'd been in each other's arms. For her own soul's sake, she'd have to keep him away. He was a tyrant who'd use any means to have his own way.

Beloved tyrant.

She hitched her purse over her shoulder and opened the door to Professor Ternan's office.

No, she must not succumb to her beloved tyrant again.

Joe dumped the scarcely tasted frozen dinner into the garbage can.

He'd never tasted one of the damned things before, and he certainly wouldn't again. So much for that alternative to cooking. How did they manage to dupe people into thinking such food was fit for human consumption?

He opened the cupboard and took out a bowl and box of Rice Krispies. Even milk, sugar, and cinnamon couldn't make it taste like more than a hurried breakfast.

His discontent with his own dinner was increased by the aroma coming from downstairs. Stuffed peppers! Damn! Beth had done that on purpose. Getting even for his issuing another ultimatum this morning. But deep inside he knew Beth wasn't capable of such manipulation.

He hadn't been able to stop thinking of last night. All day long the memory of Beth's body opalescent in the soapy water had tormented him. He thought with a physical longing of how things used to be between them. The smell of good food cooking and the laughter of the children was part of it, too. It had all been so *right*. But there was no use brooding.

Abruptly, he rinsed the bowl and spoon under the tap, went into the living room, and switched on the television. There was some inane situation comedy on about a divorced couple. The wife was big-heartedly planning a wedding for her ex-husband and her successor in her own living room while the three children watched.

Stupid rotten world! Angrily Joe switched the channel.

Beth would be leaving for her night class soon. Night class! She'd been happy before all this college stuff had come up. She'd worn her contentment like a shining garment. Too bad they didn't have another baby. Beth *loved* babies. She'd still be staying at home, taking care of their baby.

And then she wouldn't have slipped away from me yet! The thought startled him at first, but as he pondered it, he realized he'd always expected her to go someday. He'd just never quite believed his good fortune. Their life together had been too perfect. But nothing lasts forever. He'd almost consciously tried to keep her dependent on him. If she hadn't believed she could take care of herself, she wouldn't have gotten all these notions about not living with him. She'd said something about staying with him because she *wanted* to, not because she *had* to.

Well, then, how come they were separated?

He heard the doorbell ring downstairs and supposed it was Jenny Krouse, the baby-sitter. He went to stand quietly at the top of the stairs to listen. Beth was giving Jenny instructions about storing the leftovers from supper. Then she said good-bye to the kids and left.

Joe hadn't paid much attention to Jenny until she'd begun baby-sitting while Beth went to her night class. Then he'd decided he just didn't like her. For one thing, she was a fresh kid. She said she wanted to be a veterinarian. What the hell kind of profession was that for a girl? Her pets were the scourge of the neighborhood. She'd had a pet lamb tethered in the backyard, possums, baby skunks hundreds of hamsters, guinea pigs and the like, and even a ferret that had escaped and made the elderly Stoyer sisters apprehensive for weeks.

Dismissing Jenny Krouse from his mind, Joe switched on the evening news and sat down with a sigh.

About ten minutes later, Cindy came bursting through the door, her eyes glowing with excitement.

"Daddy, Daddy, Daisy's going to have a labor, right now!"

"What's that, honey?"

"Daisy's going to have a labor."

"You mean Daisy's in labor?"

"Jenny says so. Daisy went down in the cellar and lay down on Josh's bedspread that he spilled cocoa on after supper and took down to the basement for Mommy to wash. She's sort of whining."

"Who, Jenny?"

"No, Daddy." Cindy's voice was patient. *"Daisy."*

"My God! We'd better *do* something!" Joe bounded off the sofa, thrust his feet into his shoes, and ran down the stairs, Cindy at his heels.

He almost fell rounding the curve on the cellar stairs, leaving behind one of his untied shoes. The other two children were kneeling on either side of Jenny at the edge of the bedspread. Daisy was stretched out on it, breathing stertorously.

"Have you called the vet?" Joe said anxiously.

Jenny looked up over her shoulder.

"Are you for real, Mr. Columbine?" she said in disbelief. "No, I haven't called the vet and I haven't boiled any water, either. You been watching too many movies."

Jenny was a big, handsome girl with flaxen hair that hung in two pigtails. She wore faded blue jeans with a plaid patch on the seat and a navy blue T-shirt that said, "Mauled by the

Nittany Lion." Her feet were bare, which irritated Joe unreasonably.

"I suppose you know all about it," he snapped. "Look at that poor dog. She's suffering the tortures of the damned."

"Oh, for Pete's sake! She's just dilating. It's hard work, you know. It's going to be fairly easy for her, though. I think she's going to be expelling one soon."

"Will you stop that? The kids shouldn't be seeing this."

He thought in horror of his own deep fright in the delivery room when Cindy had been born. Beth had always had long, difficult labors. Something about a barely adequate pelvic capacity, the doctor had said. But Cindy had presented forehead first instead of crown first, and Beth had struggled valiantly and futilely to deliver. It had been the worst experience of his life, watching his wife in such pain and not being able to do a blessed thing to help her. The doctor had begun talking of a cesarean section when his partner, an older, more experienced O.B., had managed to get the baby turned to the proper position. Beth had finally been delivered, but not until after hours of suffering. Joe felt sweat starting on his forehead as he recalled that day. Now here was Daisy — in the vet's own words, too young to be a mother — and the kids watching. He couldn't stand for them to see Daisy's pain.

"Hey, Mr. Columbine, the kids are getting a first-class lesson in biology. Great, huh, you guys?"

The children all nodded enthusiastically. They watched Daisy, their eyes wide with excitement. Daisy's abdomen contracted hard, and a shiny, wet bit of puppy showed at the birth canal opening.

Joe couldn't tell if it was forehead or crown. "Get upstairs and call the vet, Jenny," he demanded.

"What for? You'll have to pay for a house call. Daisy's doing just fine. And if she gets into any trouble, I'm here. I guess I must have delivered thirty pups, and I can't even count the number of hamsters. Mothers usually do just fine on their own."

Daisy moaned softly and the opening widened. Joe felt all the helplessness of watching Beth struggling to bring forth their baby. Natural childbirth, hell! Those fool doctors wouldn't be so casual if *they* were feeling all that pain. Daisy whimpered, and he fancied she looked at him in appeal.

"Take it easy, girl. You'll be all right soon. Jenny, go upstairs and take the kids with you."

"You're out of your mind, Mr. Columbine," Jenny retorted. "There's nothing to be upset about. The kids aren't."

With an effort, he tried to calm down. Jenny seemed to know what she was talking about. Maybe he was scaring the kids more than the situation warranted. But he couldn't take the chance of having something go wrong. "Jenny, call the vet," he repeated more reasonably.

The baby-sitter shook her head and started for the stairs. All at once he heard a thump and a great whoosh as Jenny sprawled awkwardly on the landing.

"What happened, Jen?" he cried anxiously, reluctantly leaving Daisy's side to go to her aid. The children, too, ran to Jenny. For a moment they all seemed to be scrambling all over each other. With a rueful expression Jenny pulled herself into a sitting position and examined her knee, which was scraped and bleeding.

"Your shoe is what was the matter," she said accusingly. "I fell over your shoe and cut my knee."

"Oh, Lord! Josh, go get some antiseptic and a Band-Aid," Joe said contritely, retrieving his shoe and putting it on.

"Can't, Dad, we used 'em all. Mom put 'em on the grocery list. Does it hurt bad, Jenny?"

"Naw, it's okay, only I don't want to get dirt in it. Since you're here, Mr. Columbine, I'll just run home to get a Band-

Aid. If the puppies come before I get back, just wipe them dry with a clean rag and put them in a dry box with some soft old rags to lie on. Give Daisy a drink when she's done and bring them all upstairs where it's warmer."

"You don't have to come back, Jenny," Joe said, casting an anxious eye over his shoulder at Daisy. "I'm sorry you fell."

She struggled to her feet and started, stiff-legged, up the stairs. "It's okay. Don't worry about the kids or the dog. They'll both be okay. Honest."

He turned back to Daisy, who was whimpering softly. A puppy seemed to be stuck; Daisy's pains were futile. Just like Beth's.

"Katie, run upstairs and call the vet," Joe said, struggling not to let his worry show.

"But Jenny said she'll be okay without the vet, Daddy."

"Let's just be sure, Katie, okay? Go call him. The number's in the back of the book where Mommy writes things for the baby-sitter."

Kate nodded and ran upstairs. Joe heard the sound of the telephone being dialed, but he couldn't hear Kate's voice. He waited a minute. "Katie, did you get him?" he called. Another contraction seemed to be starting on Daisy's abdomen. She yelped once, and the puppy popped free, like a cork from a bottle.

"It's someone saying, 'I am out of my office. At the sound of the tone —' "

"Never mind, Kate. Come down and take Cindy upstairs. She's going to be sick."

"I am not, Daddy," Cindy said indignantly. "It's very interesting."

"*I'm* going to be sick!" Joe murmured. He did feel a little nauseated. He was relieved, though, now that at least one of the pups was safely delivered. Remembering Jenny's suggestion,

61

he stepped carefully around the dog and went in search of a box and some clean rags.

"Daddy, come here, quick! Daisy's laying puppies like eggs," Cindy yelled delightedly.

Joe grabbed a handful of rags from Beth's rag box, then dumped the remaining ones onto the laundry room floor and went back to Daisy and the children. The dog grunted again.

"Seven!" Josh shouted exuberantly. "Hey, look, that one's almost all white!"

Joe gave up. There was no point trying to keep the children from watching now. They were lined up, leaning forward, watching intently as Daisy brought forth an eighth puppy.

Joe spread an old towel in the bottom of the box and picked up one of the puppies gingerly, drying it off and depositing it in the box. The children were eager to help. Soon all eight pups were mewling softly in the dry box.

"I'll carry the box upstairs, kids. Jenny said Daisy should have a drink when it's over. You get her a bowl of water, and I'll come back down and carry her up."

"How will we know when it's over, Daddy?" Cindy asked.

Daisy grunted once more and something spongy and red came out. The placenta, Joe thought, feeling queasy.

"It's over, honey," he said with heartfelt relief.

It hadn't been easy getting the kids to go to bed. They'd hovered over the box, naming the pups for Snow White and the Seven Dwarfs when he had determined they were seven males and a female. Daisy was resting comfortably in the kitchen. Now, near collapse, Joe poured himself a double Scotch and soda and sank down on the love seat to wait for Beth.

At last he heard the old station wagon park out front. Beth

came up the walk and onto the porch, letting herself in with her key.

"Jenny?" she called softly.

Joe didn't answer. Beth came into the living room. Her eyes flew wide at the sight of him.

"Where's Jenny?" she asked.

"Never mind that now. Where the hell have you been? You were needed at home," he said sternly.

"Is something wrong?" she asked anxiously. "The children?"

"*They're* all right, but poor little Daisy's had a terrible time."

"The puppies?"

"Yes. She's in the kitchen with eight new puppies, no thanks to you."

Beth threw him a puzzled look and started toward the kitchen. The children came running down the stairs.

"Daisy's had eight little puppies, Mom," Josh yelled happily. "You shoulda' been here. It was neat!"

"My goodness," Beth said faintly. "Let's see."

They all trooped into the kitchen. Daisy lifted her head wearily and wagged her tail.

"My goodness gracious, Daisy, what have you got there?" Beth cried softly, her eyes shining. She knelt and patted the dog's head as if in approval. Daisy licked her hand gently. "Oh, the precious little things." Beth stroked the silky heads with a slender finger.

Joe stood in the doorway, watching his family bent over the box full of dog and puppies. A lump formed in his throat at the tenderness of Beth's gesture. He wouldn't have blamed her if she'd wanted to drown the unwanted puppies, but she'd always been kind and loving, even though she hadn't wanted the responsibility of a dog. He downed the rest of his drink and put the glass on the sink.

"Come on, kids, I think we'd better let the little mother get some rest," Beth said warmly, herding the children out of the kitchen toward the stairs. Joe followed as she kissed them good night and shooed them to bed.

She turned to Joe. "Where's Jenny?"

"She hurt her knee and went home to fix it," he said. "It's okay. I just called to be sure she was better, and her mother said it was only a scratch."

"I'm glad it wasn't serious."

He nodded. "Me, too. But damn it, Beth, it could have been. You should have been here!"

"Why me? Daisy isn't *my* dog."

"All the same, you're our children's mother, and you should have been here."

"You're our children's father, and you *were* here."

"But Jenny, a seventeen-year-old girl, was responsible for them at the time. You didn't know I wouldn't go out. You never should have left a seventeen-year-old girl in charge."

"Nonsense. Jenny could have delivered *me* if necessary!"

"She's a fresh brat and I don't like her," he said stubbornly.

"Why, Joe Columbine, I don't believe that," she said, surprised. "You liked her just fine until I started leaving the kids with her while I went to my night class. Anyhow, it isn't important whether you like her or not. The children do."

"She's fresh," he persisted "She laughed when I told her to call the vet."

"Well, everything seems to have worked out fine without him."

Unable to disagree, Joe gave an exaggerated sigh and ran a hand through his hair. Beth's breath caught as his shirt stretched across his broad chest. He looked so good in the tight blue jeans slung low on his narrow hips, with his thick hair mussed.

He raised dark eyes to hers and gave a tentative, rueful smile. "I'll get her spayed, Beth, as soon as the pups are weaned."

"That's a start. But if we're to make this joint custody work, you're going to have to accept the reasonable arrangements for the kids' care that I'm able to make."

"Good Lord, Beth, they're my kids, too."

"I'm glad you remembered. You'd have thought they were only mine when I started this class and needed someone to stay with them. When I asked you to help, you refused."

He stared down at his clenched hands. "All right, you win. I'll look after them."

"You should have been doing that all along. They're your responsibility, too, Joe."

"Okay, okay, I guess you're entitled to rub it in a little." He sighed elaborately. "I admit, I tried to keep you home by refusing to help you, and it failed. But this separation is a whole new ball game. There's no sense in paying that cheeky baby-sitter when I'm here. After all, who could look after children better than their own father?"

Beth stifled a gasp. That was exactly what she'd said to him when she'd started back to school. Wisely, she refrained from pointing that out. She contented herself with a short nod of agreement.

"The kids will certainly be pleased with that arrangement," she said honestly.

"It's settled, then. In fact, why don't you let me worry about cooking dinner on your class night from now on?"

She hesitated. Joe could take care of them, but he was hardly a cook. He grinned suddenly, as if reading her mind.

"Well, I can *learn*. And until I do, boxed chicken on Tuesday nights won't make them die of malnutrition. Only one night a week. Then you could spend the time before your class studying. You could eat with us, too."

She was deeply touched in spite of herself. Over the past winter, she'd mastered the art of providing a good meal on short notice by cooking doubles and freezing part, but now Joe was actually offering to *help!* It occurred to her that they were acting more like a team — like a *family* — than they had in a long time.

"Thanks, Joe, I'd appreciate that very much," she said simply.

He stared down at her, smiling tenderly. She felt a strong, almost visible bond between them. He looked so tired. She wondered if he'd had that stricken, pitying, helpless look when Daisy was laboring that she remembered so tenderly from her labor with Cindy. He was such a gentle, tender-hearted man. She was sorry he'd had to be home when the puppies were born. She smiled softly.

Joe moved tentatively toward her.

Oh no! She retreated visibly. No way was she going to end up in bed with him again.

"Good night, Joe," she said gently.

His expression lost its warmth as he hesitated for a long moment, then turned and started up the stairs.

"Sleep well, Beth," he said without rancor.

4

Beth worked each day until noon and spent the afternoons caring for the big house and cooking for the children. But as May wore on, it became clear that Professor Ternan's book, for which he had a firm August deadline, wouldn't be completed when school was out. In their initial agreement Beth had stipulated that she would quit working when school ended until the kids returned in the fall. Later, when Professor Ternan asked her to continue working each day until 2:10 P.M., she'd readily agreed. She'd barely had time to get home before the children arrived from school, and she'd often found herself doing housework into the evening. But she'd managed, glad to accommodate her boss, who'd been so understanding of her domestic responsibilities when he'd hired her.

Indeed, although she hadn't mentioned it to Joe, who was inclined to jealousy anyhow, one of her friends had told her the bachelor professor was something of a ladies' man. But he seemed a perfect gentleman where *married* women were conceded.

"That's a relief," Beth had said with a laugh. "I sure couldn't cope with a boss who chased me around the desk, and Joe would probably start a fight with him!"

Professor Ternan *had* been wonderful to work for. Never, in any way, did he say or do anything inappropriate. Thinking of her friend's remark, though, Beth had refrained from telling the professor that she and Joe had separated.

May was drawing to a close when she arrived for work one

67

morning to find Professor Ternan already at his desk, wearing a rumpled blue sweat suit. Beth stared at him in surprise. He was usually so smartly dressed. He returned her stare from puffy eyes.

"Is something wrong, Professor?" she asked.

"After nearly nine months of working for me, you still call me Professor occasionally," he said dully. "C'mon, Beth, you know I hate that."

"Sorry. What's the matter, Tim?" she amended with a grin.

"It's the chapter on geodesy," he said dolefully. "Wouldn't you think I'd have less trouble explaining the science of our own earth to knuckle-headed freshmen than the science of the heavens and seas?"

She nodded sympathetically. "I've noticed that part is giving you trouble. Maybe because it *is* so logical to you, you keep assuming your freshmen readers know as much as you do. Then you find you've got to explain basic tenets at a complicated stage in the chapter's development. We'll get it. How long have you been here?" she asked, glancing at the coffeepot, which was almost empty.

"Since midnight. I couldn't sleep for worrying about the book, so I got up and came in to work."

"I'll make fresh coffee and maybe we'll be able to iron out some of the tangles."

He shook his head and stood up, stretching.

"No way, Beth. I've reached the point of no return. I've got to get some food. Come on, we're going out for breakfast."

"*You* go. Surely, you have something ready for me to work on after spending most of the night writing."

"Boss's orders. Breakfast," he insisted. He handed over her purse. "Besides, I have to talk to you."

She shrugged and followed him outside.

They walked across campus to the quadrangle, then followed

the wide path down to College Avenue, which was swarming with students wearing springtime cutoffs and T-shirts, and entered the revolving door at the Cookoo's Nest restaurant. They took a booth by one of the huge windows. The restaurant's morning specialty was sticky buns and coffee. Beth sniffed appreciatively. Since Joe had been gone, she'd been using instant coffee, not caring enough to brew fresh coffee for herself alone.

She ordered the specialty, and Tim had that as well as a ham omelet and tomato juice. She savored the delicate pastry and fragrant coffee as he ate, worrying aloud between mouthfuls.

"I never should have put off this last chapter until the end," he complained. "I *knew* it would give me more trouble than the others. You tried to tell me, too."

"It'll be all right. We've nearly finished with the rest of the book. We'll make it, Tim," she said, trying to reassure him.

"*You* could make it if *I* could manage to get my part of it finished," he replied glumly. "As it is, even with the extra hours you've been working, I'm not going to finish before your children get out of school."

"There's still a week or two to go; they don't get out until June seventeenth," sale said helpfully.

"Beth, I can't see any way we can finish before the end of June. Maybe even into July." He pushed his plate away and drew his coffee mug toward him, staring at her expectantly.

"Perhaps I could get someone to stay with the children for an hour or so in the afternoon. That would give us a little more time," she suggested hesitantly.

"No, I have a summer class to teach this year. Actually, I've been trying to think of a way to ask you if you'd consider working a few hours each morning through June and, if necessary, into July."

Beth frowned and stared into her coffee.

"Tim, you'll recall that, even at the risk of being turned down for the job, I was quite open with you in the beginning about my determination to work only when my kids were in school."

"I know it, Beth. And the very first summer, here I am, trying to talk you into changing your mind," he said contritely. "Believe me, I have no intention of trying to back out of my commitment to you by threatening to let you go or anything like that. I've told you honestly all along that you are by far the best secretary and editor I've ever had." He grinned engagingly. "You know, yesterday I got a letter from my publisher saying they're amazed at the great improvement in my writing style since the last textbook. They've only got the outline and first chapter; they're going to be delighted when they see the completed book. And it's all because of you. No, Beth, I won't change the original agreement if there's no way you can, but my publisher *insists* on the August deadline. It would mean so much to me if you would help me make it. I'll pay you for the time, of course, and I'll give you a five-hundred-dollar bonus as well."

"I'd rather have a line of credit in the introduction," Beth blurted, then stared at him, embarrassed by her outburst.

He looked startled. Then he laughed. "How about both? You didn't think I'd publish the book without so much as an acknowledgment of all your help, did you?"

"You mean it? You really intend to mention that I was a real help to you? More than just as a secretary?"

He smiled at her obvious excitement. "Indeed, I will! You knew nothing about the subject when you started with me, but you've got a fantastically quick mind, and I'll say you deserve full credit making sense of my technical mishmash." ,

"*That* tempts me," she said honestly.

He stared at her, obviously perplexed.

"Beth, you never struck me as the kind of woman who cared about recognition in that way. Why does being publicly acknowledged for this work mean so much to you?"

She flushed and pushed the last bite of sticky bun with her fork. "Well, I . . . I'll tell you, but please don't laugh."

"Never," he said kindly.

"Well, I've been working on an outline for a book myself. Only a novel, of course, but being given a line of credit in your book on a complicated subject like geophysics will surely be some recommendation when I query an editor. I understand a query letter is indispensable when trying to sell a novel."

"You've been working on a book? Why, Beth, you amaze me! But what do you mean, 'only a novel'? Lord, I couldn't write a novel if my life depended upon it."

She smiled ruefully. "Only time will tell if I can. I suppose I'm insane to think uneducated old me could write anything publishable."

"What's education got to do with it? You're more educated right now them some of the college graduates I know. It takes talent, Beth, and hard work. You've already demonstrated to me that you've got lots of editing talent, and you're certainly not afraid of hard work. What's the novel going to be about?"

"Oh, no big significant theme. Just a romance set in the period of King Arthur. There've been so many excellent Arthurian novels I suppose I'm crazy to attempt another one. It's bound to seem lilliputian in comparison to the giants who've already done them."

"Listen, historical novel addicts don't mind. After all, there's nothing new under the sun. And each author's style provides the freshness they look for. Bravo."

"I realize how hard it will be to get anyone to take me seriously. I'm just another housewife pounding out a romance while the washer's on spin. But being able to claim honestly that I served as your editor on a learned textbook . . ." She shook her head, smiling proudly.

"Well, geophysics textbooks are a long way from novels about Camelot, but who knows? Maybe it will help," he said. "Does that mean you'll work for me this summer?"

She frowned. "Will you give me the line if I work for you?" she asked a little belligerently.

He laughed. "I said I'd give you the credit. Why are you so angry?"

"I'm sorry, I didn't mean to be prickly. It's just that I'm so used to being manipulated, rewarded when I do what . . . people want me to do."

"*I've* never treated you that way," he said defensively, studying her intently. "Who has? Joe?"

"I didn't say that."

"You haven't mentioned Joe lately, Beth. Is it because of him that you're hesitating to work for me this summer? Right now, you look as if you'd like to run."

"My private life really has nothing to do with our working relationship," she said stiffly.

He sat back, holding his hands up in front of him. "Hey, Beth, we've been friends so far. I'm not trying to pry."

"I'm sorry, I really am. It's just that I'm not good at dissembling. I can't hide from you that there have been . . . problems at home. In fact, right now Joe and I are separated."

"I *am* sorry," he said honestly. "If ever I heard a woman's love for a man in her voice, it was in yours. I suppose I should have realized something was wrong when you stopped talking about Joe. But we've been so busy on the book, you haven't really talked about much of anything else."

"It's all right. You were only trying to get me to work for you," she said dully.

"Yes. And I have to admit I'm still hoping you will. I'll be honest. If you say no, I'll still give you full credit as I planned in my introduction, but" — he grinned suddenly — "without you here to edit it, it may not sound so good. And your job will still be waiting in September when the kids go to school. But I really do need you. If you can find some way to manage this for me, I'll work out a better schedule next year so you won't need to go through this again."

Beth toyed with her fork, her forehead creased. It *was* a perfect job. She was aware that not many would permit her such flexibility. Although he'd assured her she wouldn't lose it if she refused, his very decency made her reluctant to let him down. He really *did* need her help if he was to deliver an acceptable book by August. She grinned suddenly.

"I guess I'll have to unless I want you to mess up my reputation as an editor," she said.

"Bless you!" he cried, leaning forward and kissing her on the forehead. "I had no idea how I'd ever make it without you. And you seem to be as good a mother as you are a secretary," he said, looking at her with interest. "I know it's none of my business, but just what went wrong with your marriage?"

"You're right, Tim, it *is* none of your business," she said quietly. "Besides, it would be impossible to explain."

"Forgive me, I was out of line. But may I ask where Joe is living?"

"Upstairs in our third-floor apartment."

"You're kidding!"

"No, I'm not. It was the judge's solution, and it's proving a practical way for us to share custody. We'll probably continue it after the . . . divorce."

"Has it really gone that far?"

"I'm afraid so."

She put her napkin on the table, self-consciously aware that her personal affairs were taking Tim's entire attention now, which embarrassed her deeply.

"I didn't mean to pry, Beth," he said again. "But if you ever need a sympathetic friend, I hope you'll consider me."

She got up and walked toward the door, effectively cutting off any further discussion. Her employer paid the bill as she went out into the soft spring day. *Damn Joe,* she thought angrily. Although Tim had always been friendly and businesslike with her, she was suddenly aware of his reputation. He "liked the ladies," was the way the gossips phrased it. Now that he was aware of the separation between her and Joe, would his manner toward her change? She fervently hoped not. She had enough to deal with without receiving unwelcome attention from her boss.

Beth peeled potatoes, onions, and carrots and placed them in lightly salted water. In an hour she would add them to the beef roasting in the oven. She'd asked Jenny to come see her after school.

When Jenny arrived, Beth poured her a glass of milk and put a plate of chocolate-chip cookies in front of her, then made herself a cup of tea.

"Jenny, I wonder if you'd be willing to baby-sit for a few hours every day when school lets out, at least through the month of June and possibly a little way into July."

Jenny dunked a cookie into her milk and bit it off thoughtfully, propping her head on her hand. "Gee, Mrs. Columbine, I'd have to give that some thought."

"Well, I guess it might be a little hard for you since you'd have to get up as early as you did during the school year. But I'd probably be home by noon."

"It isn't that, it's just . . . well, would Mr. Columbine be around?"

Beth gazed at her in confusion. "Of course not, Jen. He'd be leaving for work about the same time I would. That's why I'd need you."

"Well, if he's not going to be around, I'll think about it."

"I don't understand, Jenny. Why would his being around make any difference to you?"

The girl bit into another cookie. "He's a crazy person, Mrs. Columbine. He made me feel like I was peddling dirty pictures to the kids because I hadn't chased them away when Daisy was having her pups."

"Oh, Jenny, I'm sure he didn't mean to do that," Beth said loyally. "He's just sort of uptight about birth. I think it's because he remembers all the old wives' horror stories from when he was a kid." She knew it was because she'd had trouble with Cindy, too. She'd tried to get him to leave when things got rough, but he'd refused. A sort of melting tenderness for him made her smile. "I'm sure he was just concerned that something might go wrong for Daisy and upset the kids," she added.

Jenny sniffed and nodded.

"You real sure he doesn't think I'm some kind of weird kid or something?" she asked. "Since the night of the puppies, you haven't called me to baby-sit. I thought maybe Mr. Columbine objected to me."

"Oh, Jenny, that's my fault. It's just that he's in the house now, as you know, living upstairs, and he's willing to look after them at night when he's here."

"He wasn't looking after them before the puppies came, though."

"That has nothing to do with you, Jen," Beth said, not quite truthfully. "You see, the terms of our legal separation are that we are to stay in this house in separate quarters but share custody of the children. I think he's just taking it quite seriously."

Jenny nodded again, as if accepting her explanation. She reached for another cookie and eyed Beth shrewdly.

"You know, Mrs. Columbine, it's none of my business, I guess, but this is the weirdest separation I ever heard of. Did you know the whole town's talking about it? Those guys in the breakfast club down at the doughnut shop are laying odds that you won't get back together."

"Oh, heavens, no, I didn't," Beth said, embarrassed but amused in spite of herself. "But it doesn't much surprise me. Those men would lay odds on whether the sun is going to come up tomorrow. What are the odds?" she added mischievously.

"Two to one that you won't. But I've been taking some bets and I expect to make some money, too. Hey, Mr. Columbine looks at you as if you were a hot fudge sundae with extra whipped cream. In fact, I'd lay odds that you'll be back to normal before the summer's out."

Oh, I hope you're right! Beth thought passionately.

"Then you'll come to baby-sit, Jenny?" she said after a pause.

"Yeah, if you're sure it's okay with him. I don't want to be where I'm not wanted."

Beth assured her she would ask Joe. Jenny drained her milk glass, picked up two cookies as she stuffed her feet back into the loafers she'd kicked off and went out the back door.

Beth decided there was no use putting it off. When she heard Joe's key in the front door and his steps ascending the stairs, she put the vegetables into the roaster around the meat and went into the living room to tell the children she was going upstairs to talk to their father.

They grinned at each other.

"There's no reason for those silly smiles," she said crossly. "I just have to ask him something."

Joe answered her knock with a cooking fork in one hand.

76

She heard meat frying in the kitchen.

"Something wrong, Beth?" he asked, his expression inscrutable.

"No. Well, not exactly. I'd like to talk with you a minute, but I can come back after you've eaten."

"No, that's okay. I'm just frying a chop. I'll turn the heat down. Would you like a drink?"

"No, thanks, I just had iced tea."

He motioned her to the sofa and she sat down awkwardly as he went into the kitchen. The living room looked nice. The neat appearance was in stark contrast to the sloppy condition their house had been in after she'd begun working and before Joe had moved out. For a while she'd wondered if he was cluttering it deliberately. He could be the most maddening man.

He returned to the room and gazed down at her. "You look beat, Beth," he said, not unkindly.

"I am sort of tired," she admitted, inordinately pleased by the concern in his tone.

He reached out and touched her cheek gently. "Poor lamb, it's all too much for you, isn't it?"

She felt her throat constrict. Don't fall for that phony concern, she warned herself, and drew back from his touch. He looked hurt.

"I'm not trying to start something again," he said quietly. "It's just that you have that tense, rigid look around your jaw and neck. First thing you know, you're going to have one of those tension headaches. Try to relax."

She knew he was right and consciously tried to ease her jaw and neck muscles. Joe dropped onto the couch beside her and turned her back to him. He put his hands along her shoulders, his thumbs stroking the corded muscles of her neck. The warmth and sureness of his hands and the scarcely discernible trace of the soap he favored soothed her senses. Yet a warning kept sounding in her mind. She tried to pull away, but he held her fast and drew her back.

"Take it easy," he said gruffly. "I'm only going to massage away the stiffness."

In spite of herself she felt her body ease and loosen as his strong hands moved across her aching shoulders and neck. They were as comforting, as gentle as they'd always been, and they eased her heart along with her shoulders.

"That feel better?" he asked softly.

"Mm-hmm," she murmured languorously, wanting the moment never to end.

"I always did know what was good for you, didn't I?"

His voice sounded close to her ear. She felt his breath stirring delicately on her ear lobe, so faint she couldn't be sure it wasn't his lips she was feeling. She stiffened. As if that was a signal to Joe, he *did* kiss her ear, no mistake about it this time, then the nape of her neck. As surely as if the nerves in the back of her neck had been connected to the pit of her stomach, a delicious, familiar warmth began spreading. She tried to draw away, but his arms went around her from behind, and he buried his face in her hair. She thought she heard him sob.

He turned her until she was lying cradled in his arms. As if mesmerized, she felt her arms go up around his neck as she stared up into his darkened gaze. His eyes closed slowly as he took her lips, tentatively, gently. For a long moment their lips clung, and Beth's hand went surely to the side of his face, savoring his fine jawline and the way his hair curled around his ear. His kiss was as dear and warm and comforting as it had been a dozen times a day for nine years. Her own lips trembled under his, wanting to communicate how moved she was, how much she loved him. Her other arm went around his neck, stroking the back of his head, and his embrace tightened. All they had ever been to each other they acknowledged freely in their touches — friend, comforter, mate, confidant. He was so infinitely dear. Her Joe.

Suddenly they were no longer seeking comfort. Always, their emotions, their physical responses to each other, had been miraculously synchronized. As Joe's mouth became more demanding, hers became more yielding. He challenged her, then insisted. Beth felt herself pulsating, clinging, in danger of being swept away. If they were to make the separation work, they had to accept the fact that they were relinquishing their physical relationship. It had to be all or nothing, she thought in panic.

She pulled her arms away from his neck and forced them against his chest, trying to free herself. But Joe held her more tightly, her hands imprisoned against his chest. She felt his heart hammering furiously. His lips fluttered across her forehead, eyebrows, cheeks. He captured her earlobe between lips that felt like hot velvet. She moaned. His lips moved along the line of her jaw and, reluctantly, almost against her will, she tilted her head back to allow his lips and tongue to find their determined way down the column of her throat. How incredible that such delicate kisses could send such shattering feelings through her. Her separation from him increased her longing to a wild clamor. It was like the first time he'd aroused such feelings in her; as though, together, they were discovering the secret wonders of the world. His lips moved to the V of her blouse and, still holding her hands imprisoned, he managed to free one hand to unfasten the first button, exposing the top of her breasts above her slip.

She wanted him so much that she couldn't think. Yet deep inside, desperate to be recognized despite her longing, sanity clamored to be heard. With her last bit of strength she pushed him away and pulled herself painstakingly to the far end of the couch, where she rebuttoned her blouse.

"No, Joe, we just can't do this," she said, panting.

"Why not?" He smiled dreamily and reached for her again. His eyes were deep and soft. She saw her own reflection in them. When Joe looked at her that way during their lovemaking, she was sure she could walk right into his eyes and become part of him.

"Why not, Beth?" he said. "I thought you were a liberated woman. We've all got *needs,* you know. Yours appear to be as strong as mine."

She felt as if he'd hit her.

"Maybe it was only lust after all," she said miserably.

"What are you talking about?"

"The magic in your eyes. I always thought I could go right on in . . . oh, never mind. I thought a lot of nonsense. It seemed to me to be pure, shining love in your eyes; but we both know you don't feel *that* for me anymore, so it must be lust."

He stood up angrily. "Damn, I'm tired of your constantly analyzing all my feelings, all my actions and motives! What if it is lust? You were enjoying it."

She stood up, too, and stalked off to stand in front of the window, not wanting him to see the tears in her eyes.

"You have told me a hundred times . . . in the old days . . . before all this . . ." She motioned with her hands to indicate the apartment that represented their separation. "You told me that lovemaking wouldn't mean a thing to you with a woman you didn't love. Yet your technique's as good as ever. The expression in your eyes that I took for love — it's just part of your plan to get what you want!"

He stood in silence. With an effort Beth mastered her expression, even managed to reach up and dash the tears away without drawing his attention.

"Well, now that you've pointed out what a cad I am, maybe you'll tell me what you came up here for," he said at last.

She stared sadly at the leaves of the sweet gum tree that

80

stretched clear past the third floor, making the apartment living room seem to hang suspended. The death of a dream hurt so badly. Finally, suppressing a sigh, she turned to face him.

"Professor Ternan wants me to work in the mornings all through June and possibly into July," she said dully. "He has an important deadline, and we can't possibly finish the book before school's out."

"Well, I can't imagine you're asking my *permission*," he said sarcastically.

"No, I'm not," she replied, forcing herself to ignore his tone. "I'm going to do it. But I have to arrange for the children to be properly cared for. Jenny says she'll look after them, but she wants to be assured that it's okay with you. She thinks you consider her a weird kid — her words — because she didn't chase the kids away when the puppies were being born."

"She *is* a weird kid," he snapped.

"Joe, she isn't, and you know it."

"Well, she's damned cheeky." He thrust his hands into his pockets and glared at her. "So that's why you came up here prepared to fool around!"

She gasped, fury rising in her heart. "How dare you! *You* were the one who came on to *me!*"

"Poor baby! You *hated* it, huh?" he said with deep sarcasm.

"What's that got to do with it? You are the most impossible, conceited, arrogant, manipulative —"

"Don't forget chauvinistic! Oh, don't forget chauvinistic, Beth, that's one of your favorites," he taunted.

"You're that, too," she retorted. "But that's beside the point." She clenched her hands and fought for control. "The thing is, I *need* Jenny. No matter what you think of her, she's dependable and the kids love her. I don't worry when she's here. But she wants to know you don't disapprove. And after you tell Jenny you don't, you'd better start apologizing to me for the rotten implication you just threw at me."

"*What* implication?"

"That I would come up here prepared to . . . to . . . have sex with you just to get you to reassure Jenny. There's a very ugly word for what you accused me of, Joe."

"Oh, what's the big deal?" he drawled. "You always get so dramatic over every little thing. So what if you did? We both liked it."

"Damn you, Joe!" She strode angrily past him, heading for the stairs, but out of the corner of her eye she saw the frying pan smoking on the kitchen range. With a cry she dashed into the kitchen and pulled it off the heat, burning her hand a little. Joe's pork chop looked like an oversized licorice jelly bean. She opened the kitchen window to let the smoke out.

"My supper's ruined," Joe cried, staring at the charcoaled meat. "It's all your fault."

"*My* fault? Because you can't fry a simple chop?"

"You distracted me!"

"I didn't ask you to let yourself be distracted!"

"The least you could do is invite me down for that beef I keep smelling."

"Not on your life! No matter what kind of a low opinion you have of me, my roast beef's not for sale, and neither am I."

She stalked past him, quivering with anger.

"Beth, I . . . "

She whirled and faced him. "You what?" she cried.

"I . . . I . . . nothing. I guess you'll just have to get yourself another baby-sitter."

"And you'll have to get yourself another pork chop," she yelled, slamming the door behind her.

5

Joe tried to ignore the delicious aroma of roasting beef and the more elusive scent of apples baking with cinnamon, which dissipated rapidly as Beth slammed the door and the overwhelming smell of burned pork chop won out. Joe turned on the tap and thrust the frying pan, chop and all, under the flow, causing a sizzling cloud of steam to add even more grease to the spatters above the stove. Swearing angrily, he reached under the sink for the bottle of heavy-duty cleaning liquid he'd rapidly learned he often needed in the kitchen. Beth had always kept the house immaculate, and he was finding he could no longer abide his own clutter.

He poured the degreasing compound into the frying pan and stomped off to the living room, where he flopped onto the sofa that Beth had just vacated. He could still feel her warmth, still smell — or imagine he did — her English lavender cologne. His anger increased.

When the judge had directed that he move into the apartment on the third floor, Joe had scrupulously discouraged the children from entertaining any hope that he and Beth would get back together. But now he realized that he himself had supposed, however subliminally, that they would. Beth had always teased him about being a romantic Italian, but when you got right down to it, his realism, not his romanticism, had prompted him to imagine they'd reunite.

Their families had been friends back in their hometown, and he'd watched Beth grow from a pretty child into a beautiful woman. He'd loved her ever since he'd known her, although before she'd grown up, it had been as a little sister. He could still remember the sense of wonder he'd felt when he came home from college to discover that his "little sister" had become a ravishing and delightful young woman. In an instant he'd fallen completely, irrevocably in love.

She'd felt the same. In fact, when he declared his love for her, she'd grinned with beguiling impishness and said, "My goodness, Joe, it certainly took you long enough to get around to recognizing it. I've been crazy about you for years!"

He'd stared down at her, his joy at hearing her admission bursting in his heart. Her eyes had glowed with happiness, and the impish smile had become tender as she waited with a dignity far beyond her years for him to embrace her. He swallowed convulsively now as he remembered. That was Beth; she'd always waited for him to take the lead. She'd had a quiet, appealing confidence in her own attraction for him; she'd never run after him. He'd liked that. He'd been somewhat in awe of her, though. She was like a madonna, for all her youth, with an air of unassailable purity. It had been an earth-shattering delight to discover that she was also wildly passionate.

"It's because you're such a tender lover, Joe," she'd whispered with the tears that always came to her in moments of great joy.

He hadn't felt tender; he'd felt as if he was hurting her the first time. But they'd always responded to each other's touch with pure lightning. God, he wanted her now. He leaned back on the couch and hit his fist into the palm of his hand. Damn it, the night the bat got in, she was too upset to be blamed for what had happened, but why had she allowed him to massage her shoulders just now if she wasn't amenable to welcoming him back into her life and bed? He deliberately stifled the tiny accusing voice that reminded him *he* had assured her he meant only to ease her tension.

He thrust his feet out before him, resting them on the coffee table, and stared morosely at the tips of his shoes. He was hungry, but his stomach felt touchy. He was probably flirting with an ulcer. He thought lugubriously of what his kitchen had to offer — a small head of lettuce and half a cucumber, a frozen pizza and half a box of rice cereal. He grimaced. What a menu for a poor guy suffering from an incipient ulcer.

What did Beth want from him anyhow? He'd offered to pay her tuition. She wouldn't need to work then, would she? Even though he didn't know where the money would come from, he'd find it somehow. Maybe by cutting back on lunches downtown and taking better care of his clothes. Beth always hollered when he changed the oil in his good slacks; he *had* ruined more pairs that way than he'd like to count. Maybe he could save enough money to pay the tuition. He knew Beth could find ways if he let her do the budgeting. But by refusing the tuition money without an honest explanation, he'd started a mess.

If he'd just used a little common sense, Beth would have been happily filling the hours when the kids were in school with a few college courses and homework. Vaguely, he remembered her saying something about outlining and writing a novel. He hadn't realized she was into writing to that extent. He shook his head in wonder. She had a strength and perseverance he'd never suspected in all their years together. Lord, in the beginning she'd been afraid to make a deposit at the bank! Now she was holding down a responsible position. He had no doubt she was worth her weight in gold to the "prof," as he always called Beth's employer to himself.

The guys at the breakfast club had said Professor Ternan liked the college girls; they'd teased Joe subtly, trying to get a rise out of him. He'd only smiled, but the thought that Beth

85

was prettier than any college girl he'd ever seen, and as young-looking, tortured him. Why wouldn't she come home where she belonged now that he was willing to pay her tuition? She said it was a matter of principle. Well, he had principles, too.

With all his heart, he believed a good husband took care of his wife and, if he was able, supplied all she asked for. Didn't Beth realize he had never wanted to do anything but that? She should have known he'd have paid the tuition if he'd had the money.

He realized guiltily that she would have known if he'd explained it.

But if she truly loved him, she'd have known without his explaining, he thought illogically, and got up to make himself a salad.

Downstairs, Beth hung up the dish towel and debated the wisdom of having Katie carry a plate of food upstairs to Joe. It was tearing her apart to put the good food into refrigerator cartons while Joe was upstairs tired and hungry. He *loved* apple betty.

But if she sent him dinner, he'd take it as a sign of concili-ation, just as he obviously had when she'd gone up to ask him to reassure Jenny. She set her jaw in an angry line and put the leftovers into the refrigerator. She had too much to do to worry about Joe. There was a new baby-sitter to line up in case Jenny refused to come without Joe's approval. Jenny was a good kid, and Joe knew it. He'd often laughed good-naturedly at her breezy goodwill and her cheekiness. He'd never been angered by those traits until Beth had begun employing Jenny so she could work and go to school.

You're as bad as he is. You really ought to swallow your pride and send him his dinner, she thought with uncompro-mising self-accusation. Determinedly she pulled the leftovers out of the fridge and took pans off the rack above the stove to heat them.

The doorbell rang. She heard one of the children answer it. In a moment Cindy's voice, sounding quavery and uncertain, called "Mommie-e-e" from the front hall. Still holding a saucepan in her hand, Beth went to investigate.

Mandy Ferguson, the big, good-looking woman who worked at Springfield Realty, was standing there with a grocery bag in her arms. Beth had met her at company picnics and office parties, and she thought fleetingly that Joe had once said Mandy had a reputation for being "hot to trot," as the breakfast club boys called it. He'd even teased her a little about Mandy.

"Aren't you worried about me working with an antsy lady like that, Valentine?" he'd asked, stroking her hip.

She'd only snuggled closer against his chest and laughed. "Uh-uh. She's not your type."

"How do you know what my type is?"

She'd tickled his ear with the tip of her tongue. "I know," she'd replied enigmatically.

He'd laughed then and rolled over to imprison her and tickle her. "Yeah, you know, all right. I like a little bit of a thing with big eyes and white skin and breasts . . ."

"I'm sorry to be bothering you, Mrs. Columbine," Mandy was saying, looking a little embarrassed. "I can't seem to find a separate door to the upstairs apartment."

"*Our* upstairs apartment?" Beth asked stupidly.

"Joe's," Mandy corrected her, almost apologetically. "I've brought some things to cook him dinner."

Beth's whole body seemed to dissolve in hot water. She had a sensation of drowning, and a ringing started in her ears that spread throughout her body until she thought she was vibrating. She recognized the feeling as shock, which was rapidly turning to anger. Joe must have called Mandy after their fight, she thought in pained fury. She wanted to launch her small body at the handsome woman on her front doorstep, but after all, if Joe had called her . . . And what woman, even a "hot to trot" Mandy Ferguson, would come to a man's apartment uninvited, knowing it was where his wife lived? Probably Mandy had expected there to be a more private entrance than the front door. For one searing moment Beth felt capable of striking Joe.

"It's . . . it's upstairs," Beth said, breathing with great difficulty. "You have to come inside." She made no effort to admit Mandy, who smiled confidently and stepped up into the hall, forcing Beth to move back.

"If you'll just tell your little girl to show me the way, I won't bother you any further."

"My little girl has homework to do," Beth said stiffly. She pulled Cindy close, aware of the other children watching in stricken silence from the living room doorway.

"I guess I can find the way myself," Mandy said breezily. "Third-floor apartments are usually on the third floor." She brushed past Beth and started to climb the stairs.

Beth threw an agonized look at her children. Did they understand the implications of Mandy Ferguson's visiting their father in his apartment? Her anger and pain made her blink hard, and she realized that her hands on Cindy's shoulders were shaking.

"You okay, Mommy?" Katie said anxiously.

Beth nodded firmly, though she wanted to tear and rend and kill. How could Joe *do* such a thing? Still, she would protect the children as best she could.

"She probably had to bring him some papers from work," Beth volunteered brightly, but she could tell that the kids weren't fooled.

"In a grocery bag?" Josh scoffed. "Mom, that lady's hot stuff!"

"What did you say, Joshua Columbine?" Beth cried, shocked.

"That's what the big guys say. I don't say that, Mommy," he said defensively.

"What do you think that means?" Beth patted Cindy's shoulders and released her.

"I guess it means she likes a lot of guys, even married ones," Josh said, wrinkling his brow. "Guys that belong to some other lady."

"I hate her; she's disgusting!" Kate burst out and threw herself into her mother's arms.

"Don't, sweetheart," Beth said, biting back her own angry tears. How could she keep up her determination not to turn the children against him if he behaved like this? Good Lord, what had been going on during the six weeks he lived at the Bantry House if Mandy was visiting him right under their own roof? Katie's shaking body against hers made her forget her own pain in a white-hot blaze of anger. Suddenly she knew exactly how it felt to want to shoot one's husband. Never in her wildest nightmare had she imagined Joe could do anything like this. Beth had to restrain herself from racing up the stairs and ordering them both out of her house.

But what good would that do? The harm had already been done. The children, innocent as they were, had realized it wasn't right for Mandy to be upstairs with their father.

Katie stopped crying and rubbed furiously at her eyes, then stared at her brother and sister. "We're not going to let her stay up there," she said stoutly. "We're going up! Josh, go get the Monopoly board. Cindy, go get two puppies."

Cindy's eyes twinkled mischievously. "I'll get Snow White and Grumpy. And *no* old towel to hold under them in case of . . . you know. I'll let that lady hold them."

Beth felt laughter bubbling up inside her. She knew she

ought to restrain her children, but if Joe had really called Mandy to get even with Beth, he deserved anything they did.

Upstairs, Joe jumped at the knock. He grinned happily. Beth must have come back to make up. He fell over himself getting to the door to admit her.

To his surprise and chagrin, Mandy Ferguson was standing there, smiling broadly, a grocery bag in her arms. She wafted him a kiss and pushed her way into the apartment, taking a bottle of wine from the paper bag as she threw him a droll and suggestive smile. Joe's mouth dropped open.

"Mandy! What are you doing here?"

"It's no secret you're estranged from your wife, Joe," she said frankly. "And hey, I said to myself, you're a good-lookin' man, and I made a big enough chicken divan casserole for two, and why not? You've been looking a little peaked to me lately." She smiled and nudged him. "Not enough of that good home-cooking, good-looking." She laughed brightly and pushed through to the kitchen, setting down the wine and starting to empty the bag.

Joe stared at her in horror. He'd thought all the stories about Mandy had been exaggerated. The guys at the breakfast club liked to brag. Now here she was, acting as if she was all set for a cozy little tête-à-tête. Good Lord! If Mandy was here, Beth or one of the children must have let her in! Poor Beth! What she must be thinking? He had to get rid of this fool woman right away, but first he had to reassure Beth that he hadn't called Mandy just to punish her for not giving in to him.

"Mandy, I really don't think this will work out at all," he said stiffly. "Please don't think I'm not grateful that you went to all the bother of bringing food, but I'm not interested. I've already eaten."

He followed her glance at the small wooden salad bowl on

the kitchen drainboard with a smidgeon of wilted lettuce still clinging to the edge.

"Doesn't look like much of a supper to me," she said in amusement. "Besides, it's been my experience that men can always find room for a little more."

"Mandy, excuse me, I have to make a telephone call. Please pack up that stuff and be ready to go when I come back."

Without another word, he sprinted for the telephone in the bedroom.

He dialed and waited impatiently until he heard Beth's voice.

"Columbine's," she said dully.

"Beth, for goodness sake, I didn't invite this crazy broad," he whispered.

"I can't hear you, Joe. Can you talk a little louder?"

"You know damned well I can't."

"Shouldn't you be with your guest?" she asked sweetly.

"Damn it, Beth, now's no time to be smart. You're making me mad."

"You want to hear about *mad*, Joe?"

"Later, I swear you can be as sarcastic as you want. Right now, I have to get rid of her, and it looks like it won't be easy."

Beth seemed to explode into chuckles all at once. He could have sworn she sounded relieved. He grinned. It was okay; she believed him.

"Don't worry, Casanova, your kids are on their way to the rescue."

He heard the receiver click, and she was gone. He went back down the hall just as the children burst through the door at the top of the stairs. Mandy had opened the wine and was curled up with her shoes off at the foot of the couch, sipping some from a water glass. Another filled glass, presumably for him, stood on the coffee table.

"Ready to play Monopoly, Daddy? You promised, remember?" Josh said with a broad, conspiratorial wink.

Joe almost burst out laughing, but Mandy was frowning and looking a little puzzled.

"Hi, kids, put the game on the coffee table."

"Your father has company tonight, children," Mandy said stiffly. "Why don't you go back downstairs. Besides, he hasn't eaten yet."

Cindy glanced at the kitchen table, which was visible from her spot at the end of the couch. "It looks like my daddy won't eat it. What do you call that?"

"It's chicken divan."

"Is that in a casserole?"

"Yes, it is," Mandy said with elaborate patience. "But there's only enough for two."

"If it's in a casserole, my daddy won't eat it. He calls casseroles 'ladies' luncheon food,'" Cindy said, shaking her head adamantly. "And we don't like casseroles either so you can have it all," she finished generously. She dropped a puppy onto Mandy's lap. It promptly nuzzled her glass. She sat stiffly, holding the glass out of reach, staring distastefully at the puppy.

"You be the banker, Daddy," Kate said, taking the top off the game box. "Here, use this footstool to hold the money."

"Want to play, lady?" Cindy asked innocently.

"That's what I had in mind," she hissed in an undertone, "but not Monopoly!"

"Here, Daddy, you always take the cannon for your marker," Josh said, putting the cannon on GO.

"I want the racing car," Cindy chimed in.

"Oh no, you don't. The racing car is always mine," Josh countered. Cindy stuck her tongue out at him and settled for the hat.

"Well, then, I get to roll first," she said.

"Okay, since you're the baby. Wait, we're not ready yet."

Cindy whirled around to stare at Mandy. "You're not 'lergic to dogs, are you?"

"Not that I know of."

Cindy looked disappointed. "Well, that one there's a boy, and he's called Grumpy. The other's a girl, and her name's Snow White."

"But we could always change her name. Mandy would be nice," Kate said sweetly.

Joe stared at her in disbelief, fighting to keep a straight face. How had his sweet Katie come up with something so instinctively vicious?

"That's a great idea," Cindy cried. "She doesn't wet on people near as much as the others."

Mandy pushed the puppy hurriedly toward Cindy. She stood up, knocking the Monopoly markers onto the floor with her rainbow-hued skirt.

"I've got to be going," she said curtly. "I feel out of place at a *family* party."

Joe held her gaze. "Any parties I ever have are family parties, Mandy," he said quietly. "I'm really sorry you didn't understand that."

She smiled without rancor and stepped into the kitchen, where she packed the casserole and wine bottle back into the paper bag. She picked up her purse and walked to the apartment door.

"See you at work, Joe," she said as she let herself out. "Sorry you didn't like my . . . cooking."

Joe heaved a sigh of relief as the door shut behind her.

"Thanks, guys, I didn't know how to get rid of her."

"You didn't invite her, Daddy?" Katie said, her face lightening into a smile.

"Of course not!"

"We knew you didn't, Dad," Josh said, scuffing his sneaker

on the rug. But he looked as relieved as Katie.

"She's not *near* as pretty as Mom," Cindy said with satisfaction.

At a sound, Joe turned to see Beth standing in the doorway. Their eyes locked. Beth's showed traces of the pain Mandy's arrival must have caused her, but she was smiling.

"Kids, go downstairs and turn the oven on to two hundred degrees and put the beef and apple betty in to warm. Daddy'll be down in a minute to eat them."

The children gave a cheer and obeyed with alacrity. Beth took the wine Mandy had poured for Joe and dumped it and the remnants of Mandy's glass down the sink. The action made her feel good. Joe was standing in the doorway, watching her. He put his hand out to her and she took it, letting him lead her into the small living room, where she sat down on the rocking chair — not the sofa — effectively distancing Joe.

"I'm really sorry about that, Beth," he said. "I almost keeled over when I answered the door and saw Mandy."

Beth stared at him balefully. "Are you sure you didn't give her some inkling that she'd be welcome?"

He shook his head vigorously. "No, Beth, I wouldn't do that."

"Not that I have anything to say about who you take up with, I suppose," she added spiritedly. "But I'd never stand for you seeing a woman with our children right here under the same roof." She dug her fingernails into her palms to keep her steady. Whether she had any say or not about who Joe "took up with," the very thought of it made her sick and angry.

"I haven't taken up with anyone, Beth," he said patiently, "and I don't plan to. I can imagine how upset you must have been when you saw her. I'm sorry, and I want to make it up to you."

"How do you plan to do that? Treat me to a magic night in my bed?"

"I said I was sorry, and it really wasn't my fault."

"Nothing's ever your fault, Joe," she snapped, the sorrow of the past weeks while he'd been gone catching up with her all at once. "Everything would be all right if it wasn't for me getting uppity, wouldn't it? You're sorry about the stupid things that wouldn't have happened if you hadn't walked out on me."

"What do you mean, walked out on you?" he shouted, the color rising in his face. "You know damned well you *threw* me out."

"I asked you to leave if you weren't sure you love me," she amended miserably. "You lost no time packing your things and complying."

"Am I going to hear about that for the rest of my life, Beth? Haven't you ever gotten mad enough or hurt enough to say something terrible like that?"

"No. There isn't anything you could possibly do that would make me say something like that to you, just to hurt you, which is why I think you did it. But I'm trying, Joe. I'm trying to learn that kind of meanness. I will have achieved my goal in life when I can look at you and say I don't think I love you." Even to herself, her voice sounded bitter and cold. The effect on Joe was instantaneous and extreme. His lips went white, and he looked as if she'd hit him.

"Don't say that, Beth," he said with deadly quiet. "I can't stand to hear you talk like that."

"Why not?" she cried, fighting angry tears. She realized that Mandy's visit hadn't been his fault, and she wanted to stop yelling at him. She hated herself for being so cruel. But the pain of his remark all those weeks before came back over her as catastrophically as it had then. "It hurts, doesn't it, Joe?" she taunted. "It's the greatest pain there is, hearing someone you care about saying a thing like that."

She heard the children clattering back up the stairs. They burst through the door, their dark eyes troubled.

"Stop it, stop it, Daddy and Mommy," Cindy sobbed. "You said you were going to get a divorce because you wanted to stop fighting. But we heard you yelling at each other again."

Beth took her youngest daughter into her arms, bitterly ashamed of her outburst. "It's okay, honey," she said comfortingly.

Katie sighed deeply. "I don't think this joint custody thing is going to work," she said sadly.

Joe's eyes were filled with pain and worry. "It has to," he said in a rush. "I don't think I can stand not seeing you every day." He reached out and drew Kate and Josh into the circle of his arms as Beth continued to hold Cindy. He looked at Beth appealingly above the children's heads. "We'll stop fighting, won't we, Beth?" he beseeched. "I don't want to be separated from any of you, ever again." His eyes locked onto hers; she knew the emphasis on the "any" had been deliberate. He was telling her he wanted to be with her, too. Her heart stirred absurdly.

She inclined her head in agreement. The children hugged him.

"Beth, I'm going to do everything in my power to make our lives together work out," he said, standing up, his hands resting on two children's shoulders. "I'm going up the street right now to tell Jenny I'm glad she'll babysit for you so you can help the professor finish his book this summer. And that she can call me at work since I'm nearer home than you will be if she should need anything."

She nodded silently, deeply touched by his sincerity. Maybe there was hope for them yet. The children's eyes were large and luminous.

"You should eat first, Daddy," Katie said. "The food ought to be warm by now."

"No, honey, when I make up my mind to do something, I want to get it over with. I'll be back soon." He turned to Beth. "Will you have a cup of coffee with me while I eat?" he asked gently.

The tightness around her heart began to ease a little. It felt so much better to be talking with Joe than shouting at him. She was sorry she'd lost her temper, sorry to have misjudged him, but so happy, she realized in a rush of relief, to know he hadn't invited the amorous Mandy to his apartment.

"I would love to have a cup of coffee with you, Joe," she said honestly.

6

Their tandem lives settled into a workable routine as spring wore on. Beth treated Joe with elaborate courtesy, not wanting to disturb the tenuous balance of their new relationship and aware that he was going out of his way to be accommodating. She was as content as she could be under the strange circumstances of their separation, and delighted to see that Joe seemed happier and more relaxed than he had been at the Bantry House. Now that he'd stopped hassling her, she was more than ever aware of his sweet charm that had won her heart, and she was certain he was feeling a grudging respect for the way she'd accepted responsibility for her own life.

Professor Ternan contracted a virus that laid him low for three days, providing Beth with an unexpected vacation from work. She used the time to good advantage, getting the children's summer clothes out of storage and taking their winter clothes to the dry cleaner. She chafed, though, when several days of rain kept the soil too damp to plant the small garden she kept each summer. The many flower beds, now riotous with spring blooms, would need to be weeded. The lawn was ankle-deep from the heavy rains, and the mower needed to be tuned up. She knew Joe would see to the mower and the grass, but she'd always done the garden and the weeding. She thought briefly of asking him to handle these tasks for her this summer, but discarded the idea. There was no point in rocking the boat.

The morning of the children's spring concert, Beth was

cleaning the kitchen cupboards when the telephone rang. It was Professor Ternan.

"Are you feeling better?" she asked.

"Barely," he replied gloomily, "but I just had a call from my publisher demanding what I've done so far on this final chapter. I'm going to have to get it off to them by tomorrow morning or they're threatening to delay publication for a whole year."

"Do you want me to come in?"

"There's no use today," he replied. "I don't have anything ready for you to edit and type. But I'm going to crawl out of bed, pour a gallon of coffee and cough syrup into me, and work here at home all afternoon. I'll need you to come in for a couple of hours tonight. I'm sorry, Beth, I really am. I know how you feel about being with your children at night, but I'm desperate."

"But tonight's their concert. Cindy's first, in fact. I just *have* to be there."

"For heaven's sake, Beth, you're not going to damage their little psyches by missing one concert," he said, and sneezed violently. "I have to insist," he added miserably. "I *can't* risk not having the book out for next year's term. You do understand, don't you?"

For a desperate moment she was tempted to quit. She could hear herself saying the words. Joe would be so happy. Indeed, *she* would momentarily feel a freedom from tension. She could get caught up with the housework, give more time to her studies . . . Joe *had* promised to pay her tuition.

She wanted a reconciliation with Joe badly enough to use this incident as an excuse to effect it; it would be so easy to let the struggle go, to slip back into Joe's protective arms — in effect, to let him have his way.

But she couldn't do it.

Moreover, her basic decency wouldn't allow her to leave

Tim high and dry with his book uncompleted. She sighed in resignation.

"Okay, I'll be there. What time?"

"Bless you, Beth. Say five-thirty? Figure on giving me at least four hours. Thanks, you're a peach."

Beth frowned as she hung up the receiver. A peach, all right. What would she do about the concert? Maybe Joe would be willing to go with the children and listen to their selections, although he never had before. He hated concerts of any kind.

But she dreaded telling him she would be working tonight. Lately he'd been accepting her job and school better than she'd ever thought he would, but she was afraid to push him too far. Please don't let him be angry and alienated again, she prayed. Please let the new-found peace and respect between us continue.

As she passed through the front hall, Beth saw Joe getting out of the car and coming up the walk to join the children, who were playing jacks on the porch step. She hadn't realized it was so late. She'd have to ask him to accompany the children when he came in. He looked up toward the eastern sky and smiled, pointing and saying something to the children, who looked, too, their faces wreathed in smiles. Joe glanced up and gestured for her to join them outside. She pushed open the door.

"Oh, Mommy, it's a rainbow," Cindy cried. "It's the most beautiful one I ever saw."

"We learned about rainbows in school last winter," Katie chimed in. "They're caused by the reflection of the sun on many, many raindrops at different angles."

Joe reached out to take Beth's hand. "Do you remember the rainbow after our first quarrel?" he murmured.

Beth nodded, remembering only too well. "The rainbow is caused because all those raindrops are acting as mirrors and

100

prisms, just like the prisms I have in the windows to make the house full of rainbows," she said trying to ignore the pleading in Joe's eyes. Remembering the early days of their love was entirely too painful when they couldn't seem to resolve their present differences.

"Do you mean a rainbow can only happen after a rain, Mommy? When the air is still full of raindrops?" said Cindy.

"Yes, honey, that's right."

The little girl stared at the rainbow in awe. "Then I will never hate the rain again," she said quietly.

Beth could feel Joe's intent gaze on her. Reluctantly she lifted her eyes. His lips softened in a smile. "Maybe we should feel that way, too, Beth," he murmured. "I feel . . . something dazzlingly wonderful —" He broke off in confusion, inarticulate again, almost as if he were embarrassed. Could he truly be working his way through all his reservations about her new independence? She waited, watching him quietly, wanting him to reassure her that he was ready to accept a marriage in which they were equal partners. He seemed about to say something when Josh broke the silence.

"Mommy can't come to the concert tonight, Dad," he said. "How about it? Will you come?"

"Well, I don't know. You know I don't like concerts."

Beth's heart sank. "But I can't go this time, Joe," she said quietly.

"Why not?"

"I have to work for about four hours tonight. Professor Ternan has been sick for three days and has to catch up. His publishers are insisting that he meet this latest deadline. It won't happen again. What about the concert, Joe?"

The children were staring at him expectantly. Joe frowned. She knew he didn't like her to work at night. But at last he sighed and rumpled Josh's hair.

"Okay, you guys."

Beth let her breath out in relief. "Thanks, Joe," she murmured. She knew he was making a real effort.

It just wasn't in him to hurt his kids or disappoint them more than he could help.

Joe finished shaving and took his shirt and necktie from the bathroom doorknob. He put them back on, drawing the knot of the tie snugly into place, and stared at his reflection in the mirror. Boy, he *must* be getting mellow. He couldn't believe he'd actually agreed to attend the kids' concert. He hadn't even said much about Beth's working tonight.

Downstairs, Katie tootled one last, quick rendition of "The Rainbow Connection" on her flute, although she had said the band director had told them not to worry about practicing on the day of the concert. Katie the perfectionist.

Beth had already gone to work. Joe grimaced at his reflection. His stomach contracted in the now-familiar spasm that he'd come to recognize as meaning he was scared. There, he'd thought it. He was scared that Beth would find someone else and sever all ties with him.

He'd seen pictures of Professor Ternan accompanying write-ups about books he'd had published or lectures he'd given to various organizations. He was one of those good-looking, confident, arrogant types you expected to wear Harris tweed jackets and excel at skiing. He was also a bachelor. How could a sweet, innocent woman like Beth keep from having her head turned by such an important man telling her how indispensable she was to him? And how could the prof ever keep his hands off Beth?

Joe thought with mingled pain and pleasure of the way her passions had surged to life under his ministering hands the night the bat had gotten in. She'd been wildly beautiful and every bit

102

as ardent as himself. Since then, there'd been long weeks of deprivation after years of frequent and satisfying lovemaking. If that . . . that egghead made a move on her — and why in the hell wouldn't he? — would she respond? The whole world had gone crazy, and Joe sometimes felt as if he belonged in another place, another time. Maybe it was true what the guys in the breakfast club kept saying: "it" was available everywhere. The whole world was into instant gratification, casual, recreational sex. Certainly he'd never dreamed Mandy would actually come to his house, with his wife and kids downstairs, all ready to go.

Beth was even less at home in this new world than he was. He hoped she was proof against the prof's charm.

Joe had been deeply disappointed that she was going to have to work tonight because all along he'd planned to surprise her by accompanying her and the kids to the concert. He didn't protest, though. Nothing must jeopardize their working arrangement. He had to be where he could see the kids every day.

And Beth, too. There was no use denying it. He needed to see for himself that his wife was all right, too. For all her conviction that she could take care of herself, she had a certain vulnerability. He felt better being on the premises should she need him.

Joe realized guiltily that he should have been going with her to concerts all along. So what if Josh sang like a beagle with laryngitis? And who cared if he'd already heard Katie's selections on the flute a hundred times? They were his kids, too. Wryly he realized he was coming to accept concerts and chicken pox as being as much a part of parenting as circuses and Christmas.

In the kitchen he dried the saucepan he'd washed and left in the dish drain. He'd managed to make passable chili con carne tonight. Maybe there was hope for him as a cook. Maybe he'd buy a cookbook, or borrow Beth's, and try making bread. He hung up the dish towel, put on his jacket, and went downstairs. Cindy and Josh met him. Katie was sitting primly on a cane-seated chair in the front hall, her flute in its case at her feet.

"Did you put Daisy and the pups in the cellar?" Joe asked. "Remember, they can climb out of the box now, and we don't want them wetting Mommy's rugs."

"They're down, Dad, and I left a pan of water for Daisy," Josh said, grinning. "You ready?"

Joe observed that the children were delighted he was going with them. He was inordinately touched.

"Ready!" he said, smiling. "Pile into the car."

"Oh, Daddy, it's only a couple of blocks. We could walk," Kate said, picking up her flute.

"Well, we couldn't walk clear uptown to the Felicity House for a sundae afterward, now, could we?" he said pleasantly.

They cheered exuberantly and ran ahead of him to the car.

Joe got in and started the motor. He had always driven the "good" car since it used far less gasoline than the old battered station wagon, which was, moreover, better for Beth to haul kids, groceries, and garage-sale acquisitions in. Perhaps, though, now that she was driving to the university every day, he ought to suggest she take the sedan. She hadn't mentioned the faulty fuel pump in the station wagon recently, he thought, momentarily concerned. Perhaps it hadn't been as bad as they'd thought.

There was so much traffic around the elementary school that he thought they'd have been better off leaving the car at home and picking it up after the concert for the drive to the Felicity House. However, he managed to park on North Allegheny Street, the first in line. Other cars quickly pulled in behind him, but he'd have no trouble getting out.

The children ran off to their classrooms, where they were to report before the concert. Joe made his way to the auditorium, smiling at acquaintances and realizing in guilty surprise that he was far from the only father in attendance.

The seats must be the most uncomfortable in America, he decided. He squirmed, trying for a comfortable position. The auditorium was filling rapidly. A lady with three preschoolers entered the row behind him, her protrusive stomach — another on the way — forcing him to lean forward in his seat. She settled ponderously into place and tapped him on the shoulder, demanding to know the time.

"Six forty-five," Joe said after consulting his watch.

"What time's the concert s'posed to start?" she asked, aiming a practiced swat at the behind of her little boy, who was straddling the back of the seat beside Joe.

He glanced at his program "Eight o'clock," he said. *Eight o'clock?* All the parents were already there; they had had to drop the kids off at six forty-five. Where were the suburban and country parents going to spend the time until the concert started except in the auditorium?

It promised to be a long evening, he thought as the boy hit him in the ear with a cowboy boot. The pregnant woman, who resembled a prizefighter, kept admonishing her kids in a booming voice.

"Jerome, you quit kickin' that man in the head, you hear? Sherilee, quit whining, I forgot your damned doll. Gregory, no, you *can't* go. I told you to go before we left home, and I don't know where the bathroom is!"

Joe thought guiltily of how little he'd appreciated Beth's faithfully attending the concerts alone. He was uncomfortably aware that the little girl who was resting her chin on his shoulder snuffling gently had consumed scrambled eggs for supper. He

105

turned to meet her eyes, and their noses bumped.

"You're leaning on my sweater, mister," she said dolefully.

Joe saw that she had somehow draped her sweater over the back of his seat, presumably when he'd leaned forward to allow her unborn sibling access to the row behind. He leaned forward again, allowing the child to reclaim the garment.

"Sherilee, put your sweater on and stop bothering that man. Can't you see he's gettin' mad at you?" the prizefighter said in the same fretful tones.

"*I'm* not getting angry," Joe said with a reassuring smile.

"Then how come you look like you just tasted sour milk?" the woman said unpleasantly.

Joe abandoned the attempt at geniality. Desperately he looked around the auditorium for another seat, but already people were standing at the back. He subsided miserably.

Much later, he applauded fifteen renditions of "Country Gardens" played on the tuba by various students who were performing in public for the first time. Joe's appreciation of Beth's solitary attendance increased. Jerome's cowboy boot connected with his ribcage for the third time.

At last Katie and two other little girls stood up in front of the conductor and waited their cue for their flute trio of "The Rainbow Connection." Joel's heart eased a little. Katie was such a lovely child, so pretty and earnest. She was going to look just like Beth. They played the piece tolerably well, and his applause at the end was wholehearted.

Then came the choral part of the program. Josh sang loudly with the second-graders, despite the conductor's determined quashing motions toward his side of the stage. Josh bowed in unison with the other kids, his eyes roaming the audience. When he saw Joe, his face split into a pleased grin, revealing the empty place where his two front teeth were just coming in.

When it was the first-graders' turn, Cindy stood primly, her

106

hands folded exactly as she'd obviously been told, her eyes never leaving the conductor's face. Her little mouth formed a perfect oval as she sang an animated arrangement of "Old MacDonald." Cindy sang the cow's part. The "moo" came out of her oval mouth very well indeed. Joe suppressed a chuckle in case she should catch sight of him.

At last it was over. The spring night was rapidly darkening as he emerged from the auditorium and looked around for his children. One by one they found him and listened as he congratulated them.

"You were great, kids, just great," he said and realized, to his own astonishment, that he meant it. Maybe they wouldn't be performing at Carnegie Hall in the near future, but their enthusiasm was hard to resist. If it hadn't been for the prize-fighter and her brood, the evening wouldn't have been too bad, Joe thought, his natural buoyancy returning.

They crossed West Linden Street to the car. Joe saw with dismay that a pickup truck had managed to squeeze dangerously in front of him. It extended out into the intersection. There was no way under the sun he'd be able to move until the owner of the truck drove off. Or until all the drivers behind him pulled out, he thought ruefully, noting that the car behind him had pulled in too close as well. He unlocked the car, and they all piled in.

"I can almost taste a root beer float," Joe said teasingly, to pass the time. "What about you guys?"

"Peanut butter fudge sundae with chocolate ice cream for me." Josh sighed happily.

"I'll have a cherry royale sundae," Katie said.

"I want Brownie à la mode," Cindy trilled.

Suddenly a crowd of children converged on the truck as a pregnant woman climbed laboriously behind the wheel. It was the prizefighter. She put the preschoolers into the cab and at

107

least one child for every grade piled into the truck bed. They pummeled each other and yelled, the mother outshouting them all. The truck roared asthmatically to life and, to Joe's shocked dismay, leaped back into his sedan with a sickening jolt and the sound of breaking glass.

Damn fool woman! "You've got it in reverse!" he shouted, jerking the door open and loping toward the driver's side of the truck. "You've smashed into my car!" In the near dark he couldn't assess the damage. The kids in the truck bed stopped pounding on each other and leaned over the edge, grinning inanely at him. "Why did you park here anyhow? There wasn't room!"

"You're crazy, mister," the woman boomed belligerently. "I only nudged your damned car."

"Nudged? Then I'd hate to be in a car you smashed!" He thought of the kids and ran back, sticking his head in to ask if they'd been hurt.

"We're okay, Daddy," they chorused. The woman started to move forward as the light on Linden Avenue turned yellow. Joe wheeled around and ran toward the truck. "Wait a minute, where do you think you're going?" he demanded. "Do you have insurance?"

"They canceled it last week," the woman yelled, gunning the car through the light just before it turned red. Joe tried frantically to read her license number, but she turned quickly onto West Linden and disappeared into the darkness.

He swore impotently and looked down at the mayhem she'd wrought. The bumper was dented in, one headlight was smashed and pushed into the fender, reminding Joe of a marshmallow poked by a child, and the grill was bent. He shook his head and got into the car.

"Did she do much damage, Daddy?" Kate asked sadly.

"Enough," Joe said gloomily. "And I didn't get her license number either. Not that it would do much good, I suppose. She said her insurance had been canceled." Of course, he had a one-hundred-dollar deductible, but he could just hear his insurance man complaining that he should have gotten the license number. He'd have to call the police and report it if he was going to submit a claim.

"Will you have to pay for it, Daddy?" Josh asked.

"The first hundred dollars, son."

"Hey, Daddy, we don't need ice cream tonight," Josh said staunchly.

"I could almost taste that brownie à la mode," Cindy said mournfully.

Josh whispered, "Shut up, Cindy!"

Joe started the car. To hell with it. The kids were going to have their treat. He could call the police from the Felicity House.

But how about that Josh? "Hey, Daddy, we don't need ice cream tonight," he'd said. What a little guy.

Joe had filled out the accident report and the kids had long since settled down to sleep. Still, Beth wasn't home. He paced the floor, looking out the oval glass on the front door for her ancient station wagon. His own accident made him uneasy. The roads were full of maniacs. Suppose someone had plowed into her?

At last a sports car with the top down, an English Triumph, pulled up in front of the house and a man got out on the driver's side. He hurried around to open the door on the passenger side and handed Beth up to the sidewalk. He dropped her arm, but accompanied her down the two steps into their yard, along the broad slate walk and up the four steps onto the big front porch. Joe opened the door. It was pointless to pretend he hadn't been

109

standing there watching.

"What happened?" he said anxiously. "Where's the station wagon?"

"Sitting in the parking lot with a fuel pump that finally refused to function," Beth said. "Tim hadn't left yet and offered to bring me home. Oh, you haven't met my boss, Joe. This is Professor Tim Ternan. Tim, Joe Columbine, my husband."

Joe smiled icily and proffered his hand reluctantly. So it was *Tim*. There was nothing to do but thank the handsome professor for seeing his wife home safely. The prof nodded and stepped down off the porch.

"Thanks, Beth," he said. "I'll see you tomorrow. We really made progress tonight."

Joe kept smiling stiffly until the professor had driven off with a toot and a wave. Then he turned to Beth. "Progress at what?" he demanded.

Beth looked at him witheringly, her hand already on the banister to go upstairs. "Joe, I think I ought to warn you, I'm in no mood to be taken to task tonight. The car wouldn't have broken down if you'd taken care of the fuel pump when you said you would. Besides, I couldn't have called you since you'd have had to leave the children alone to come for me. The buses stopped running hours ago."

"I'm sure the prof didn't mind bringing you home," Joe said moodily. "I'll bet it was romantic, cruising along under the stars with the top down."

"I really didn't notice. I was far too tired. I think you're jealous, Joe."

"No, I'm not," he snapped, though he certainly was jealous. He thought suddenly of the look in Beth's eyes the night Mandy had barged in. Had she felt like this? Had her heart felt as if someone were squeezing it brutally? She was staring at him solemnly, but he thought he saw amused pity in her dark eyes.

110

"I'm sorry you're upset, Joe," she said gently. "Please believe me, I'm not the least bit interested in Tim Ternan except as an employer." She gave an amused, self-conscious chuckle that he thought was meant to reassure him. "I'm too tired and too committed to my family . . . to y—" She stopped short, casting him a quick look.

She did look weary. There were circles under her eyes.

"Damn it, Beth," he said in sudden concern, "this is all too much for you."

To his surprise, she nodded in agreement. "I don't know how I'd manage without your help. I'll be glad when the book's done."

"Beth, maybe he's just trying to keep you near him. You're a very beautiful woman," he said in a rush.

"I shouldn't like hearing that from you so much, Joe," she said softly.

He gazed at her, longing to draw her into his arms, to let her lean against him for a while. Belatedly he realized she had spoken of commitment to her family as a reason she wasn't interested in the professor. Hadn't she almost said something even more specific about the commitment? Had she been about to say "to you"? He leaned over and kissed her full lips, not passionately, just wanting to comfort her, grateful that she was home safe.

Sighing, Beth laid her palms against his chest and let them slide up and around his neck. "I love you, Joe," she whispered so softly that he wasn't at all sure she'd really said it.

With wonder he realized he felt happy. She was here. And *safe*. If he persisted a little, let his own heartfelt desires take over, he might be able to talk her into a reconciliation right now. He wanted to carry her upstairs, climb into bed with her, and hold her all through the night, keeping her safe from broken fuel pumps and bachelor professors.

But that wouldn't be fair. He'd be taking advantage of her weariness and her love for him. His conscience was getting the better of him, he thought, grimacing.

No, Beth was coming to some kind of peace with herself as she made a new life. He loved her too much to manipulate her. He kissed her gently and disengaged her arms.

"Go to bed, Beth," he said huskily. "You're almost dead on your feet."

She glanced up at him quickly, confounded by his sudden reserve. When he'd touched her at other times since their separation, he'd either made love to her or tried to. Things had been going so well for them. These past few days he'd seemed to be accepting her as an equal, respecting her work and fulfilling his share of the marital responsibility. She'd felt reassured, especially tonight when he hadn't raised a fuss about her having to work. She knew that if he wanted her, she would have trouble refusing. She'd thought he was jealous of Tim, but it had only been concern for her welfare. What was she trying to do, embracing him like that? Sabotage their amicable separation? Joe was simply coming to terms with it. He'd mellowed greatly. Maybe the single state was agreeing with him. All at once, she was terribly depressed. She couldn't be truly, truly losing his love.

Yet, she loved him too much to interfere with his adjustment to their splitting up. She sighed and turned away.

"Will you lock up, Joe?"

"Sure, Beth. See you tomorrow."

She climbed the stairs slowly. His arms around her would feel so good tonight. She longed with all her heart to fall asleep on his shoulder as she had for nine years.

"Never again, darling," she whispered to the empty bedroom. There were tears in her eyes.

7

No longer looking ill, Professor Ternan had already arrived at the office when Beth got there the following morning. She'd had to take the bus since Joe's car had also met with misfortune the evening before. He'd told her about it early that morning and promised to have the station wagon taken in for repairs when he brought his in during his lunch break.

Tim greeted her with the warm camaraderie she imagined two siege survivors might share. She could readily understand why. His anxiety about missing the book deadline had infected her yesterday evening, so she'd worked hard, forcing herself to grasp the concepts of geophysics he was laboriously explaining with each page of manuscript. By ten-thirty they'd finally wrestled the chapter into understandable sentences and paragraphs. Today she would do the final editing and type what she hoped would be the final draft. They'd accomplished more than Tim had hoped, partly, he'd generously remarked, because she had readily understood the difficult concepts of geophysics. If they were able to work as satisfactorily on the index and footnotes today, perhaps she'd be finished working before the end of June after all.

"You look a little tired, but as beautiful as ever this morning, Beth," her employer said in greeting. "I never realized the duties you must have in your private life. Even in the dark I could see that behemoth of a house must be a woman-killer. Do you have a cleaning woman?"

His tone this morning had a new intimacy that disturbed Beth. He'd never paid her a personal compliment before, nor particularly referred to her personal life. She wanted to frown but didn't want to seem to attach any importance to his curiosity.

"So far, I've managed alone," she said shortly.

He stared at her, still smiling. "Don't shut me out, Beth," he murmured. "I thought we were getting to be friends."

"Of course we're friends," she said with a laugh.

"You know what I mean," he said softly.

She turned and met his blue gaze. "No, I don't know what you mean, Tim," she replied evenly.

"You and your husband haven't gotten back together, have you?" he said, as though the possibility had just occurred to him.

"No, but that still has nothing to do with our being friends."

"I'd sort of hoped it did."

"No, Tim, not in the least."

"You'll get back together," he said. "Who ever heard of two separated people living in the same house?"

"I imagine a lot of people live together in name only," she said. "And a lot separate without hating each other."

"You're certainly not in either category, I'd imagine."

She fitted a sheet of paper into the typewriter as if to end an unwelcome discussion.

"Look, Beth, you have to admit, I never said a word to you as long as you were happily married, so don't turn me off as if I were some skirt-chasing playboy. I'm not, you know."

She threw him a look of skeptical amusement.

He grinned. "Look, I see women every now and then. They're not serious, I'm not serious, and we both know it. Nobody gets hurt."

"You don't have to explain your personal life to me any

114

more than I have to explain mine to you." She typed the page number.

"Don't you ever think of anything but work?"

"Sure." She typed rapidly, trying to end the conversation. "Children. School. The novel I'm working on. Politics. The state of the economy. Housework."

He sat down on the edge of her desk, putting both big hands down over the page she was reading from. She stopped typing and met his eyes with a sigh.

"You didn't mention fun," he said. "Don't you ever do anything just for the hell of it? Don't you ever relax?"

She stared pointedly at the sheet of manuscript in the typewriter. "I'll relax when this book is done," she said insinuatingly. "Don't you think you ought to get started on the footnotes?"

"Okay, Mrs. Columbine, I can recognize a brushoff when I get one. Let me remind you again, though, that I never came on to you when you were happily married or at least appeared to be."

The exchange with her employer made the rest of the workday awkward to Beth, although Tim refrained from any further discussion of her separation or his apparent infatuation. That was all it was, she told herself. Tim Ternan just couldn't stand not turning his charm on every unattached woman he met. No doubt his sincere approach was custom-tailored to her own conservative standards. She'd never had the slightest experience in parrying such flirtatiousness. Perhaps it would have been better to have laughed at him. She'd just been herself, not knowing any other way to behave. By responding to him seriously, she had probably made herself ridiculous in his eyes. He was looking for fun, and she acted as if she believed everything he said. She hoped with all her heart he'd soon tire of the game and go on to someone else.

She brooded over the episode as the bus bore her homeward. She'd often been the subject of admiring glances, but everyone in their little town knew she was a happily married woman, and so she'd never had to deal with unwanted male attention. Now she was being confronted with the possibility of being forcibly thrust back into the world of two by two.

She had never once considered life without Joe — or, rather, life with anyone other than Joe. Yet if their separation continued into divorce, Joe would inevitably make a new life for himself that didn't include her. A too-familiar depression assailed her. They were moving inexorably into patterns that excluded each other.

She forced her thoughts back to the possibility of their eventual divorce. She'd truly be alone. Alone in a world where dating, mating, and trivial relationships abounded. Even now, when so many women were divorced, she'd heard acquaintances make snide remarks about divorcees they knew: "hot to trot"; needing a man to "take care of her"; "grateful for all favors." Her jaw grew rigid. Perhaps people would soon be speaking of her that way. Maybe they already were. Maybe that was why Tim Ternan had approached her.

She *did* miss the happy, relaxed physical relationship she'd enjoyed with Joe. At night she tossed and turned, unable to find a comfortable position, thinking of Joe asleep in the room above hers. How would she cope with her own hungers as the time apart wore on?

She couldn't imagine making love with anyone but Joe. That's all there was to it. Tim Ternan was attractive in the way of a poster boy, someone to inspire sighs and groans. No one ever seriously thought of such men as partners in love.

"Partners in love" had been the way she thought of such relationships. For her there wasn't any such thing as a *sexual* relationship. If having sex with a man was just a means to

116

fulfilling biological needs, it would cause her far more problems than it solved. With Joe, making love had been many things. They'd done it in all kinds of moods: sometimes playful, when they'd end up laughing over something ridiculous; often wildly, frantically passionate; at other times sweetly romantic, evocative of their wedding night. Once, after her favorite aunt had died, though she'd felt a tiny twinge of guilt at wanting to make love, it had been blessed comfort. Joe had reassured her:

"Honey, I guess when we lose someone we love, life seems all the more precious. Aunt Clara would be the first to say 'Bravo.' She loved life as much as anyone I ever knew. And the lovemaking between a husband and wife is one of the best things life has to offer."

Yes, their lovemaking had always been deeply satisfying, a logical and ultimate step in their all-encompassing love. A hundred times he'd told her it would mean nothing to him with anyone else, without the deep and abiding love he felt for her.

But he'd said he wasn't sure he still loved her. The unwelcome, nagging thought recurred, always ready to take her unawares and cause a swift, sure thrust of pain.

People did change. Never in a million years would she have believed Joe could, though — that he could come to stop loving her. But since he'd been living upstairs, she'd noticed a great deal of change in him. He was not nearly so boyish in his enthusiasms. The old, spontaneous flamboyance seemed gone forever. Since the night Mandy had been there, he seemed to have accepted their separation as a fact; indeed, she brooded about that awful night frequently, although she'd ceased placing any real significance on Mandy herself. The incident seemed to Beth a milestone in their parting ways.

The bus approached her stop. She pulled the cord and stood up, gripping the handle on the back of the seat for balance. Joe could find another woman if he wanted.

But she would never, never find another man.

On the Saturday morning before Memorial Day, Beth and the children climbed into the newly repaired station wagon for a trip to the bank and to buy groceries.

Beth had her own salary check to deposit. Ever since their separation, Joe had been giving her the amount he'd usually set aside for groceries and the children's clothing. Up until that time, he'd actually bought most of the groceries, although he'd wryly observed that Beth was a far better shopper than he.

Yet he'd so loved shopping for the children, letting them buy what pleased them, that she'd never had the heart to protest very seriously. After two months of shopping on her own, she realized grimly that they'd wasted more money over the years than she had imagined. The water heater had broken down and had had to be replaced shortly after Joe had moved to the Bantry House, and Beth had been able to pay for it out of the money he'd given her. Even such a major expenditure hadn't forced her to dip into her paycheck, which she'd largely banked for nine months. Her balance was now almost seven thousand dollars.

Outside the bank the streets were lined with tables for the Saturday morning farmer's market. Beth bought a basket of apples, a small bunch of asparagus, and, although the price was a little high, a basket of early strawberries. She'd make a cheese-cake for dessert and serve the strawberries with it. With effort she dismissed the memory of how Joe loved that dessert.

At the supermarket the children took turns pushing the cart and checking the coupons she'd clipped against the items she put in the cart. She systematically gathered all the items needed for the coming week, buying four large pork chops for supper as well as ground beef and endive for Italian wedding soup.

When they reached home, the sight of Joe weeding the flower

118

beds almost made Beth drive up over the curb. She opened the back door of the station wagon and started extracting bags. Joe glanced up and saw her. He pulled off his work gloves and dropped them on the grass, then came to take the bags of groceries out of her arms.

"I dug your garden, Beth," he said almost shyly. "It's still a bit damp for planting."

"Thank you, Joe," she said dazedly. "I really appreciate that. I'd never have gotten to it today."

She took the last bag of groceries from the car and shut the door, then walked beside him down the steps and across the yard to the house.

"If you trust me to do it right, I could plant it for you next week," he said uncertainly.

She stared at him in astonishment. "Sure, I trust you to do it right. But I haven't bought the plants yet. I guess I should have. The farmers had some nice pepper and tomato plants for sale today."

"I'll go get them as soon as I've finished the mowing and weeding. How many do you suppose I should buy?"

"Well, a dozen of each will give us all the vegetables I'm likely to have time to take care of."

She opened the front door with her free hand and held it open for Joe. He carried the groceries into the kitchen and deposited them on the table. The children watched him expectantly, as if bemused by his volunteering to do some of the chores.

Joe smiled at them and stroked Josh's hair. "You guys want to help me outside?" he asked.

"You bet, Dad. What do you want us to do?" Josh said as Katie and Cindy nodded.

"Well, Cindy could hold plastic garbage bags for me while I empty the grass container on the mower into them. Josh and

Kate can weed, unless Mommy has work for you to do in here."
He looked at Beth expectantly.

"No, that's okay," she said, trying to hide her surprise.

"Why don't we bring the puppies outdoors for a little sun, too?" Joe suggested. "Then I'll clean up the basement. They make an awful mess down there. I think I'll fix a place in the carriage house for them."

"Won't that be too cold?" Cindy asked.

"No, it's warm enough now. Besides, they're big and husky and almost old enough for us to find other homes for them. There's some lumber out there. I think we'll make a big pen in the corner of the carriage house."

He and the children disappeared into the yard to begin the hefty pile of chores he'd outlined.

Beth stared after them in amazement.

She heard the mower start outside and the children murmuring under the kitchen window as they weeded. Why hadn't they been able to work together like this without separating? She started putting groceries away.

Dear God, she prayed fervently, please let him see we could still have a good life together. But she warned herself sternly to stop fantasizing about a reconciliation.

Joe was only helping for the good of the children. After all, she thought ironically, a man had to make concessions to an estranged wife that he never would to an unseparated one. Yes, that was all his new helpfulness meant. He was doing it all for the good of the children.

Beth finished the laundry, vacuumed the house, and made the cheesecake. As it cooled, she hulled strawberries and added Italian seasoning to the meat for the tiny meatballs to go in the wedding soup. Joe had finished the yard work, done his own laundry, and taken the children along to buy tomato and pepper plants. She cleaned the endive and assembled the wedding soup, turning the heat to simmer before putting stuffed pork chops in the oven. Then, the chores finished, she went upstairs and showered, washing her hair, and dressed in a red cotton blouse and skirt. When she came downstairs, Joe and the children had returned.

"I put the plants out in the carriage house and watered them," he said. "And I picked up fire alarms to install on all three floors. Our insurance man said we'd get a discount on our premium if we installed proper alarms."

"Will it make a lot of mess?" Beth said, and could have bitten her tongue.

But Joe didn't take offense. "I don't think so, but if it does, I'll clean it up." He hesitated. "You look nice, Beth."

"Thanks," she said in some confusion.

"You also look tired. Why don't you stretch out and rest awhile?"

"Won't you need help with the fire alarms?"

"No. Piece of cake." He grinned.

She smiled back, joining him in the joke. He wasn't much of a handyman. Nevertheless, she resolutely left him to the task, following his suggestion that she stretch out for a rest.

As Joe installed the last fire alarm on the stairs just above the front hall, the mailman arrived. Smiling at Joe's obvious pride over the newly installed alarms, Beth flipped through the mail. There was a magazine, a bill for Cindy's dental checkup, and a wedding invitation.

"It's your brother's, of course," Beth said happily as she held the invitation out for the family's inspection. Much to the children's delight, it was addressed to Mr. and Mrs. Joseph Anthony Columbine and Katherine, Joshua, and Cynthia.

"Well, they're really going to do it," Beth said, pleased. They'd known, of course, that Joe's younger brother, John, had given his girlfriend Liz an engagement ring the previous Christmas. They'd planned to marry during the summer if John did well in law school and got a summer job. It must have all happened as they had hoped.

She opened the invitation and read it. The wedding was set for the last Saturday in June in their hometown near the Ohio border. The children began chattering happily about Uncle Johnny's wedding.

"We could give him a puppy for a wedding present, Mommy," Cindy piped. "Bashful or Sleepy, maybe. That way, at least one of Daisy's pups wouldn't be going to an ol' stranger."

"Honey, I think a nice check would be more useful to John and Liz," Joe said, laughing. "But we can ask if anyone in the family wants a pup."

"Speaking of dogs, do they like their new pen in the carriage house?" Beth asked the children.

"Well, we decided not to put them out there. Dad thought it might be too cold after all," Cindy said.

"But we put a door across the old coal cellar so they couldn't mess up the whole basement anymore," Josh added. "We scrubbed the rest of the basement, Mom, and Dad says we'll do the same to the coal cellar once we've found homes for the puppies."

Beth nodded. "You'd better all go down and play with them for a while," she said. "They might be a little uneasy in the coal cellar at first."

The children started downstairs. "Take the toolbox, too, Josh. I'm finished with it now," Joe called.

When they were alone, he smiled at Beth. "I can see you wanted to get rid of the kids so we could talk alone, Beth, and I think I know what's on your mind."

"Do you, Joe? I've been dreading this. Oh, not John and Liz

122

getting married, but the necessity of telling our families we're separated."

"Why will we have to tell them?"

She traced the edge of the invitation with her finger, coloring a little. She couldn't help remembering the day she and Joe had picked out their own wedding invitations. "Because we always leave the kids at my mother's house and you and I always stay at your mother's. In her guest room."

"Specifically in her guest room's double bed, you mean," he said flatly.

She met his eyes reluctantly. "Yes, that's what I mean. We can't pretend we've been living together. Sooner or later we'll have to tell them we're separated and contemplating a divorce."

"We're not going to do it, Beth."

For one wild, happy moment she thought he meant they weren't getting a divorce. She stared at him with her heart in her throat. She swallowed convulsively.

"We can't drop a bomb like that on the family in the middle of John's wedding," he continued.

Beth lowered her eyes to hide her disappointment. "I suppose I could stay home. You and the children can go. Tell your folks I had to work."

"You know darned well that won't work," he said patiently. "They'd all be so hurt. And they know there is nothing on earth that would keep you away from a family wedding."

"Do you think I could stay with my folks? Say I want to catch up on the family news with Mother?"

"You always spend about half the time with your family. We all do. The sleeping arrangements have always worked out fine. Any excuse to change them will make them wonder."

"Then what will we do?"

"About sleeping together?" She looked up quickly at his strained, almost cynical tone. "We've slept in the same bed without making love. Not often, I'll admit. What's the matter, Beth, afraid I'll take advantage of you?"

Before she could reply, the children came back upstairs and passed them on their way to the living room, where Kate turned on the television.

"We'll talk about it later," he said softly. "I'm going to take a shower."

Beth went to the kitchen and checked dinner. The pork chops were succulently perfect and big enough to feed Joe, too, if each of them cut a small part off his or hers. She doubted he'd had time to cook anything for himself with all the chores he'd done around the yard and house, and he did so love stuffed pork chops and cheesecake. She debated sending Josh upstairs to invite him down for dinner, but the thought that she might seem to be trying to coerce him into a reconciliation made her hesitate. She knew that pride made her reluctant. Life was so complicated.

As she was putting the finishing touches on the table, the newly installed alarm on the third floor erupted into a raucous din. Beth jumped in shock and fear, then froze for one split second. Not so the children. They exploded through the living room doorway into the hall, Josh taking the stairs two at a time. Seeing her small son spring into action brought Beth out of her paralysis, and she loped across the dining room and followed him up the stairs.

In the second-floor hallway they saw smoke pouring down from above.

Beth's heart contracted with fear.

"Joe!" She passed Josh as if he were standing still, turning the corner at the landing and racing for the apartment. He came running out of the bathroom at the top of the steps, dripping wet, a towel clutched inadequately around his middle. The smoke was coming from the kitchen beyond the living room.

He tore through, Beth almost on his bare heels, relief that he was unharmed making her feel weak.

A saucepan on the stove was the source of the smoke. Joe turned off the burner, opened the window, and, still clutching the towel, turned on the tap and used a dish towel as a potholder to convey the smoking pan into the sink. The running water hit it and made a cloud of steam join the smoke in hissing fury.

"I was heating a bowl of chili," he explained apologetically.

Beth slumped down onto the sofa and laughed in relief. "At least we know the darned thing works," she said.

Joe stalked out into the hall where the alarm had been installed, adjusting the towel more securely about his middle. He reached up and stopped the cacophony. Beth tried not to notice how magnificent his bare body was. She got up and opened the windows in the living room while Josh opened the casements on the landing.

"Boy, Dad, you're getting to be a pretty good yard man, but you still can't cook," Josh said, laughing nervously. He came back up to stand in the hall beside his father. Joe grinned engagingly and motioned Josh and Beth to follow him to the kitchen. He opened the oven door and, donning two oven mitts, pulled two perfectly baked loaves of bread from the oven.

"Wanna' eat your words, son?" he drawled.

"Wow! Did you make that bread, Dad?"

"You bet. From scratch, too. I borrowed your mother's cookbook while you were at the store. The dough's been rising all day."

He dumped the loaves out of their pans and wrapped a clean towel around one of them. Eyes shining with pride, he held it out to Beth. "One for each of us," he said generously.

"Only if you'll come down and eat dinner with us," she said, no longer afraid of what he'd think. She was so happy he wasn't hurt, and she felt completely disarmed by the day's events.

"Just let me shower the soap off and get dressed," he said. Josh watched them, beaming.

Beth took the proffered bread, and she and Josh went downstairs to set another place at the table.

The girls were nowhere in sight. Puzzled, she called out to them.

"Out here, Mommy." Cindy's voice came from the sidewalk.

Beth walked to the door. Cindy was sitting on the sidewalk, clutching Daisy tightly around the middle. All seven pups squirmed in a laundry basket behind her.

"What are you doing, honey?"

"Daddy told us if we ever heard the fire alarm we were to get the hell . . . to get out of the house and call the fire department. Katie's gone next door to call them. We didn't get out right away, though Mommy," she added apologetically. "We couldn't let poor little Daisy and her babies burn up, could we?"

Just then the fire alarms at the East and West fire companies went off downtown.

"Oh, no!" Beth cried, laughing. "Too late to stop Katie."

The entire neighborhood was coming to see what was going on.

"It's okay, honest," Beth cried. "We just set off the new fire alarm, and Katie got carried away and called the fire company." She was blushing as red as her blouse and skirt.

When the fire trucks arrived, she explained the mishap. The east company chief insisted on climbing the stairs to the third floor to make sure there was no danger.

At last the fire trucks went away and the street quieted down. Beth stood on the sidewalk with her children. She saw Joe pass the casement windows on the third-floor landing.

"Take the puppies back to the basement, girls, and wash your hands," she said. "Daddy's going to eat supper with us."

Their faces split into pleased grins.

"Now, don't go getting any ideas," Beth admonished, smiling in spite of herself.

As she put the finishing touches on the table, Joe watched television with the children. The blue-and-white woven tablecloth picked up exactly the blue in the dishes. She'd arranged tulips and narcissus in a pewter bowl.

Finally she called her family to the table, and they bowed their heads to say grace together. She filled their bowls with wedding soup from the tureen.

"Is this that new kind of wedding soup?" Joe asked suspiciously.

"I used canned stock, if that's what you mean, Joe," Beth said without apology.

He stared doubtfully down at it. "When did you start cooking celery in it?"

"There's no celery in the soup."

He stared harder. "That looks like celery stalks to me."

"It's only the endive stems. They seemed so young and tender, I didn't bother to cut them off."

He tasted the soup gingerly, then glanced at her quickly and ate an entire spoonful. "It's *good*, Beth," he said in astonishment.

She ducked her head to hide her smile.

If the children hadn't been there, if she hadn't been reluctant to get their hopes up, she'd have told him the whole day had been good.

Different, but very, very good.

Just as Beth said good night to the children, the doorbell rang. It was Jenny Krouse.

"Mr. Columbine called me to come stay with the kids so you could go out," she explained.

"Oh, but —" Beth began, but Joe, coming down the stairs, interrupted her.

"Get your sweater, Beth, we're going to take a walk," he said firmly.

Jenny grinned broadly and sauntered into the living room. "Take your time. I don't have a date this evening, but don't broadcast it. I have a reputation to uphold," she called over her shoulder.

Wonderingly, not meeting her husband's eyes, Beth retrieved a sweater. Joe held the door open for her as she preceded him onto the front porch.

The moon was high and seemed to sail through the windswept skies. Joe took her elbow as they went down the slate walk to the sidewalk. Then he let his hand slide down the inside of her arm until they were holding hands.

"Do you remember how we used to take walks, Beth?" he asked softly. "We'd go for miles and miles, talking so much we never realized how far we'd gone."

She smiled in remembrance. "Yes. I remember the time you took me to a perfect stranger's wedding, and we walked all the way across town afterward."

"I was trying to get you in the mood to marry me." He laughed.

"I remember walking out the old back road when I was pregnant with Katie and being so tired we had to call the neighbors to come pick us up," she reminisced. "I think I missed walking most of all when you moved out."

"More than making love?" he asked tenderly.

Beth smiled and shook her head, glad that the trees shadowed her face. "Was there some special reason you called Jenny, Joe?" she asked, aware of his hand, warm and firm, holding hers securely. "Did you want to discuss what we'll do about the sleeping arrangements at the wedding?"

"No, I most certainly do not," he said emphatically. "I just wanted to take a walk with my wife. Just relax and enjoy the evening. I'm tired and edgy, and I think you are, too."

"I am, Joe, really."

They strolled down Elm Street to Allegheny, where they turned south, enjoying the balmy evening and the soft song of insects. An occasional bat darted into view at the periphery of street lamps, attracted by insects that fluttered in the golden light.

"Maybe I should capture a bat and let it loose in your room," Joe said, his eyes caressing Beth's in the soft light.

She laughed in spite of herself and briefly rested her forehead against his arm. "Don't even joke about it," she said. "I still tremble just to think of it."

"Affected you that much, huh? I tremble to think of it, too."

"Joe! You know what I meant," she said, suppressing a smile.

They walked to the drugstore in the center of town which was still open, although only the druggist and one counter girl talked desultorily behind the soda fountain. Joe ordered milk shakes for both of them, then wandered around the store while the young woman mixed them, coming back with a beautiful crystal flagon of the lavender perfume Beth favored.

"It's a little late, Valentine, but I'd like to give you a birthday present," he said solemnly.

Beth stared at him uncertainly. Sometimes it felt as if there had never been any estrangement between them. He acted as if he wished there never had been.

"Joe, that's all right," she said softly. "Don't try to make up for things that are past."

"I have to, Beth. But I'm trying to build a better future, too."

Her heart soared. When he paid for the perfume and milk

shakes, she didn't protest. She opened the bottle and dabbed some scent behind her ears.

They drank their shakes and walked home slowly, talking softly together. It was the nicest evening Beth had had in months.

Joe paid Jenny and locked the doors. He kissed Beth good night gently and passionlessly before going up to his apartment alone.

He leaned over the railing and gazed down at her.

"I'm giving you fair warning, Beth," he called softly. "I'm going to wear you down until you agree to a reconciliation."

8

That night Beth expected to fall asleep right away; she was certainly tired enough. But at midnight she was still twisting and turning, trying without success to stop ruminating on her problems.

Why had Joe participated so conscientiously and entirely unasked in the house and yard work? Before, he had always left such tasks to her or called a repairman. Lately, he'd been spending more time with the children, too. Last night he'd even helped Katie with her homework. Beth supposed his new involvement only demonstrated a determination to make up for the separation.

Yet, he'd taken her for a walk and said he wanted a reconciliation. Could he mean it? The thought was at once exciting and comforting.

More likely, though, he was just trying to reassure the children that things would continue largely as they had before he and Beth had separated. He had always believed that parents owed their children a sense of security even more than the obvious needs of food, clothing, and shelter.

She pummeled her pillow, then wedged it under her shoulders and sat up, staring into the dark. She felt as if she hadn't had a good night's sleep since Joe had left — except for the night they'd made love. It was still hard to believe they'd ever come to this stage. With a physical longing she wanted her family to be back together again.

She and Joe had always been friends. She remembered the

wonderful magic when their friendship had turned to love. She had begun to feel it long before he had, when she was only fourteen and she'd missed him so much when he went away to college. When he came back for Christmas in his freshman year, she knew she loved him. But she nursed her devotion in silence for four more years before Joe fell in love with her, too.

She smiled as she thought about their courtship. He had taken her to the senior prom and danced every dance with her. She knew he'd felt a little silly going to a prom when he was already out of college and working for Mr. Springfield. But they'd danced to sentimental songs all night, and when they'd gone home at dawn — to her father, who was fuming about the "modern" custom of young women staying out all night on prom night — Joe had told her parents he wanted to marry Beth when she was twenty.

She'd felt wonderful and special to be given Joe's love, and Joe had assured her, with unselfconscious conceit, that indeed she was. He, Joseph Anthony Columbine, wouldn't have married just *anyone*. With all her heart, she believed there'd never been a couple more in love. They would look at each other at family gatherings, across a crowded shopping mall, over a sleeping baby's crib, and the love would be there, tangible between them. "Aren't we lucky?" their eyes would signal. "I love you so much."

She reached for a tissue. When the entire world was tearing itself apart because everyone in it was searching for just what she and Joe had — one other human being to care with all his heart and strength — wasn't she crazy to be throwing it away? Joe wasn't a classic tyrant. Twenty years from now, when she was aging and lonely without him, would it really matter that he hadn't allowed her to grow to her full potential? Did it really matter now that she yearned to do things — to learn about medieval life and to write beautiful novels? Why should wanting to create fictional worlds be so important to her? Wasn't the real here and now infinitely preferable? If she lost Joe, what did anything else matter?

She heard footsteps cross the study, and someone knocked on her bedroom door. She pulled on her robe, thinking one of the children needed her, and opened the door.

Joe was standing there in pajama bottoms and slippers, his dark hair falling over his forehead. "I can't sleep, Beth. Can we talk?"

She tied the belt of her robe and thrust the tissue into the pocket, absurdly happy to know he was as awake as she was.

"I'll make us some hot chocolate," she said, brushing past him. Her heart was hammering in spite of herself. It was all she could do to keep from reaching out and twisting her fingers in the curly hair on his bare chest as he turned and followed her into the kitchen. How incredible that he should be so close to her yet so removed. She felt his presence behind her on the stairs, knew his dark eyes were naked with longing as they bored into her back. *Oh, Joe,* she wanted to shout, *we belong together.*

She took a copper-bottomed pan from the rack above the range and mixed cocoa and sugar with a little hot water from the tap, then filled the pan with milk and put it on to heat. She took the cheesecake from the refrigerator. "Would you like some, Joe?"

He grinned. "You might be able to twist my arm."

She smiled and cut a piece, then spooned strawberries over it. No matter how complicated Joe's life became, he could always eat, she thought fondly. She put the cheesecake in front of him and poured the hot chocolate into two cream-and-blue mugs, then sat down opposite him.

"This is so good, Beth. I've missed your cooking."

She suppressed the desire to ask if he'd missed her as well. "You wanted to talk, Joe?"

133

He stared at her. She noticed that he was shivering. "You're cold. Just a minute." She got up and rummaged in the kitchen coat closet until she found a red cardigan sweater he'd seldom worn and hadn't bothered to take upstairs. He put it on gratefully. Beth tried not to think about the expanse of bare chest still revealed. She pulled her own robe more tightly about her.

"Look, I've never been very articulate. This isn't easy. I guess it's never easy to say you've been wrong."

"Are you trying to say that now?"

"I guess I am. A lot of it has been my fault, I know. I think we need to talk about it."

She met his eyes. "I tried so hard to get you to do that," she said with a catch in her voice. "Just to talk about all that was bothering you. But you . . . both of us . . . always ended up arguing."

"I know, I know. I'm as stubborn as an army mule. But I'm ready to talk now. Like a mule, I guess you've got to hit me in the head to get my attention."

"I'll talk all night if it will help," she murmured.

He smiled gently. "We used to talk all night when we'd been separated by a one-night business trip. Remember?"

She answered his smile. "That wasn't all we did."

"No, sweetheart, that wasn't all. Beth, I don't want to throw it all away."

"I never wanted to split up in the first place. But when you said you weren't sure you loved me anymore . . . Joe, you know how I am. To me, the greatest immorality in the world is to clutch someone to you who doesn't love you or want to be with you."

"Please don't keep reminding me of that," he said miserably. "I wish I'd never said it."

"Not half as much as I wish you hadn't," she replied bitterly. "Especially since you knew it was the cruelest thing you could ever, ever do to me."

He put his hand across her lips to silence her. His eyes were tortured. "Please, Beth, don't retaliate in kind. I can't bear it."

She dropped her eyes, shamed. "I'm being a spoiled brat to cling to my pain over it." She sighed. "I realize that I alone can get it back in perspective. I have to accept what happened and go on from there. I just haven't had much luck at getting over it yet."

"I wish I could change it for you, but I can't. I'm sorry."

She nodded silently.

"You must deal with that just as I have to deal with the changes in you."

"What changes, Joe? You keep saying I've changed, but I don't know what you mean. I always told you I wanted to go back to college."

"I know. And I even admit you had every right to think I agreed. I was wrong. I'm ready and willing to make up to you for that. A good man provides for his wife's needs. If going to college is one of your needs, I did wrong to forbid it. I told you the morning after the bat that I'm perfectly willing to give you permission and pay for your tuition as well. I even give you permission to work if you feel you have to."

"Are you listening to yourself, Joe?" she exclaimed. "You 'give me permission'?"

He sighed deeply. "See? That's made you mad. I'm not trying to make you angry, Beth. I told you I want to talk, compromise."

"You don't even understand why I'm angry," she cried. "Don't you realize you 'give permission' to our children? I don't need your permission."

"And you try to deny you've changed?"

She pushed her cup away, not meeting his eyes. "Maybe I have," she said slowly. "Maybe. But I think you had the wrong perception of me all those years. You thought I was obeying you by spending every moment of my life with you and the children. But I wanted to. It never occurred to me that I had no choice in the matter. You accused me of neglecting our children by wanting to develop a part of my life that had nothing to do with you and the children."

"I'm sorry about that, too. You're the best mother in the world. But I'm an old-fashioned man. You know how I was brought up. The man earns the living, and the woman takes care of the house and children. When you went to work, it was as if you were saying you weren't satisfied with the way I've been taking care of you."

"That's nonsense," she said, not unkindly. "And no one in his right mind would consider my working a slur on your providing."

"It seems that way to me."

"Oh, Joe, it isn't written in gold that men work and women keep house. But that's all beside the point anyhow. Please don't try to push this discussion back into that old theme. You said you wanted to talk. Let's really talk. It isn't school or work or whether I've changed or whether or not you've ceased to love me that's caused this problem, and you know it. It's your assumption that you, as the man in this marriage, have the right to make decisions about my life."

"You make decisions about mine," he said reasonably. "You made no secret about being upset over Mandy visiting me the other night. And you certainly had that right."

"You are being deliberately obtuse. Our very marriage vows gave either of us certain rights over the other. I'd expect you to lay down the law in exactly the same way if I had a male visitor with expectations about me similar to Mandy's about you."

Joe glowered at the very thought.

"See, Joe?" she said with mild triumph. "No matter what you say, you've done more to hurt me over this basic conflict than I have you. I'm talking about your demanding control over my basic human rights."

"When we got married, a contract was implied, Beth. I thought you were accepting it. I would earn the living, you would take care of the kids and the house."

"I've done that."

"I helped you today."

"Oh, so that's it. Do you want a medal?"

"I admit I should have been doing it for you a long time ago. I haven't been fair. The yard and washing windows and painting walls — things like that are too hard for you."

"And so you're willing to do them 'for me'?"

"They *are* your responsibility, Beth, just as earning money is mine," he said reasonably.

She sighed and put her head down on the table. He reached out tentatively and stroked her curly head. "I've been trying. Can't we get together again?"

She sat up and met his eyes. "I don't know how to talk to you," she cried. "I want to get back together. God knows I do. But I'm sure I can't live under such a basic conflict of philosophies."

"Can't we just agree to disagree? Can't you knuckle under even a little to preserve our marriage?"

"Can you?"

"I am. I said I'll tolerate your working if it's the only way."

"You'll tolerate. What if I only tolerated your working? Don't you see? What you're willing to accept is like putting a skin graft over a wound that's gangrenous. How long before the poison works its way back into our marriage and kills it?"

"You always get so dramatic. It's not that big a deal. You don't want to hear me say it, but you've been taken in by those women libbers. You think women have never achieved the success men have because they've been shackled, and that all we have to do is treat them exactly the same. But, honey, then why did the Almighty make the woman the childbearer? You can't blame men for that."

"Damn it, Joe, I refuse to get into one of those silly arguments about the women's movement again. You're deliberately simplifying the issue. I'm interested in us, you and me, not the social structure of the ages, or God's reason for designing human reproduction as He did. The human soul has no gender. I don't try to control you and you have no right to control me."

"Whatever happened to 'and the two shall become one'?"

"You don't understand! The two *shall* become one. I believe with all my heart that that means two equals join and become something new, composed of their equal parts. To you, it means you stay the same and I become absorbed in you."

"But I'm willing to concede what you want. Even though it goes against my own beliefs. Doesn't that prove I love you and want you back?"

She drew a hand wearily across her forehead. "Maybe it does. I don't know about the love. I'm afraid that if I force you to go against your own beliefs in this way, what love you do feel for me will die. I guess I just wouldn't want to win by making you lose."

He came up from the chair and drew her into his arms, deliberately forcing her face against his neck so he could speak against her ear. His strong hands held her imprisoned against his body.

"I wouldn't be losing, Beth I'd have you back."

She tried to pull away. "We'd both be diminished, Joe. Let me go. I'm so tired. I just want to go to bed."

He released her reluctantly. His brown eyes smoldered as he gazed down at her. "Let me come with you, Valentine. I'm so damned sick of being alone."

"I know," she said. "Me, too. I guess I'll never stop loving you. And I want you, too. With all my strength. You're just about the most wonderful, sweet, sexy man I can imagine. You don't deserve all this hassle, but I don't know what to do about it. I have to be true to myself. And so do you."

His eyes filled with genuine bafflement and a pained disbelief that wrenched Beth's heart. "You won't give it a try?"

"I can't. I really want to, but I can't. Try to understand. For months I've been telling myself I ought to be willing to make any concession necessary to live at peace with you. But I knew I'd be betraying my own best principles if I did. Now you're willing to do that for me, and I find I can't bear for you to betray yours."

"You accused me of wanting a perfect, fairy-tale romance, Beth. But you're the impractical one now. Nobody has a perfect marriage."

She sighed, her weariness bearing her down like a pall.

"I know. I've already been through all this in my heart. You seem to have reached a stage I've already passed through."

He smiled wryly. "Well, at least I'm making progress."

She reached up and stroked his cheek. "I have to tell you how much I admire your willingness to give in, though."

He grasped her upper arms and held her, gazing earnestly into her eyes. "I've made up my mind. There'll be no more childishness. I'm man enough to admit when I'm at fault. You've been right so far, and I'll abide by what you say. Maybe you're even right about the folly of reconciling when it's against my principles to give in on so many issues. All I know is I want you back. I want things to be the way they used to be, and I'll do anything I have to to make them so."

She stood silently in his grasp for a long moment. She could smell the faint, clean essence of him and feel the warmth of his body. The temptation to give in, to make both their dreams come true, if only for a little while, assailed her. She wanted to collapse into his arms, to put her lips against the broad chest. She sighed.

"I doubt if things can ever be the way they used to be," she said. "There's only today, here, now. Only one way through today's difficulties. Through, not back. Perhaps, if we want to badly enough, we'll come through this place and into a better future."

He stared down at her. "I'm going to try to get you back, Beth," he reiterated. "I'll use any means, fair or foul. Including this."

He pulled her smoothly into his arms again, taking her lips as surely and as expertly as if she hadn't been struggling to free herself. Relentlessly he drew her, his hands cupped around her hips and forcing her against him. She felt his response to her nearness, and her own heart began hammering with excitement. She moaned softly, gasping for breath, but he wouldn't release her. Almost against her own will, her hand slipped up and around his neck, her fingers twining in his curly hair as she drew him closer.

What was the use of fighting? They belonged to each other; they were two consenting adults. Still kissing her, he scooped her up into his arms and carried her up the stairs, through the study, and into her bedroom. Very gently he put her down on the bed and turned on the light. He drew away from her then, his breath coming rapidly from excitement and the exertion of carrying her.

But as he stared down at her, his expression underwent another transformation. He seemed to be waging an inner battle. At last his passion seemed to cool, and he sighed deeply, running a hand through his hair. His voice came quietly to her in the darkness.

"More than anything on earth, Valentine, I want to stay here with you tonight, and I think you'd let me. But later, when it was over, I think you'd hate yourself and maybe me. I'd have lost more than I'd gained."

She gazed at him in astonishment. She'd been sure there'd be no stopping him without a violent struggle. And, in truth, she hadn't the strength to resist. All the same, she was pathetically grateful for his self-control.

"Thank you, Joe, for understanding. Good night, my darling."

He stared down at her for a long time. "Good night, Valentine." He leaned over and kissed her lightly, then was gone.

During the days that followed, Beth felt they were almost a family again, except that she and Joe weren't sleeping together. He seemed almost like the old, good-tempered Joe, yet sometimes when she looked at him unawares, she detected a hard line to his mouth that had never been there before. He seemed to be holding himself in control with great difficulty. She was aware, perhaps more than he was, of the anger he was suppressing.

A subtle change had come about. Neither of them was thinking in terms of divorce. Beth knew the present arrangement couldn't go on indefinitely. The tension between them grew daily. Joe had always been a lusty man; she couldn't expect him to remain celibate.

She couldn't even call their struggle a contest of wills, she thought dismally, since Joe had offered to give in for the sake of peace and reconciliation. Still, she waited, hoping in spite of all reason that one or the other of them — at this point she honestly didn't care which — would have a true change of heart so that they could decide on the direction of their lives once and for all.

One evening when Joe returned home from work, he came into the kitchen rather than going up to his own apartment. "Can you talk to me for a minute, Beth?" he asked, sinking into a chair.

Beth's spirits rose as they always did when he sought her out this way. "Sure, Joe." She turned the heat to low under the stew and sat down opposite him.

"I have to tell you what happened today at work or I'll burst," he said, loosening his tie. "Do you remember maybe four months ago when I told you I'd made a suggestion to Springfield about keeping a file on everyone who'd called about a property and checking it periodically?"

"Yes, I remember. You said that often a house didn't work out for a person who called about it, but the very fact that they *had* called indicated they were interested in the possibility of making some kind of move."

"That's right. I always kept a small card file of people's names and the property they called about. Now, when a similar property comes on the market, it's easy to forget any individual, but if I check through this file periodically, it often refreshes my memory."

She stared at him admiringly. "Joe, that seems so logical and sensible you'd think all realtors would do it as a matter of course."

"Many do, but unfortunately not all. Anyhow, when we got the new microfiche, I started putting all the information on my little file into the fiche. You know what Springfield said? That I was hustling business. Hustling, for heaven's sake! As if there was something sordid about trying to sell the right house to the right client. He implied that his fine old family realty had never had to resort to such money-grubbing practices."

"Oh, Joe, I am sorry."

142

"That isn't all. At the sales meeting today he announced he's been giving a great deal of thought to fully utilizing the new fiche, which, by the way, I talked him into installing. He told all the realtors to get any prospective client information they had ready for me, good ol' Joe, to program into the fiche. He told the most moving version of how *he* found a property for the Withersteens because of *his* foresight in keeping a prospective client's file on them. Damn it all, Beth, I didn't expect any medals for finding the house for the Withersteens. I was only doing my job. But to have him take my ideas like that and present them as his own . . ."

"Oh, honey, that's a rotten shame." Beth said indignantly. "He's a mean, petty, nasty, penny-pinching parasite."

George Springfield had been Joe's employer since he'd graduated from college, and Beth knew Joe had doubled the man's sales volume in those twelve years. She had always realized that Springfield ground down Joe's pride in many petty ways, but this latest incident seemed the most blatant offense yet.

Joe was shaking with indignation and fury.

He clenched and unclenched his fists. Beth poured him a glass of iced tea, which he accepted gratefully. When he'd finished it, he leaned back and grinned ruefully, with an air of hard-won resignation. Thanks for listening, Beth."

"I wish I could do more than listen," she said fervently.

"There isn't a whole lot to be done. Just hope the old man retires soon."

"Do you think that will make things any better? You never much liked George Junior, either."

"No. But he's so stupid he'll probably leave us alone."

"I hope so. I hate that you're forced to work at a job that takes so much from you and gives you so little appreciation."

He put the glass on the drainboard and turned toward the

kitchen doorway. "I feel better for having talked about it. Thanks. Don't worry about it."

When he'd left the kitchen and gone upstairs Beth turned back to preparing dinner. He always said, "Don't worry about it," right after telling her something that was bound to worry her a lot.

If only Joe could get out from under the Springfields, father or son, she thought intently. If only there were some way. She wondered how much it would take to buy them out. Joe had no idea how much money she had in their bank account. Seven thousand dollars ought to be enough to get a bank loan for a down payment. She smiled at her own whimsy. Why would Mr. Springfield be willing to sell a business that kept him in comfort, especially when Joe was doing all the work?

But what if Joe were to leave Mr. Springfield? His goldmine would surely lose some of its luster without Joe Columbine. She made up her mind to talk to Joe about it.

By the twenty-second of June, sooner than they'd anticipated, Professor Ternan's book was finally finished and ready to mail to his publisher. Late in the morning Beth took the final manuscript, packed for mailing, and laid it triumphantly on her boss's desk.

"What a relief," she remarked happily. "I thought we'd never finish. It's going to be wonderful staying home all day for the rest of the summer."

He smiled warmly. "That's not very flattering. Aren't you going to miss your handsome, charming boss?"

She grinned. "Do you want an honest answer?"

"By all means."

"I'm going to miss the job more than I expected to, Tim, and I have to admit, I'll miss you, too. You've proved to be a great employer, very understanding about my family obligations. I hadn't expected to learn so much about writing in this job. I thought it would be mostly just checking your punctuation and sentence structure and then typing the final manuscript."

Tim leaned back in his chair. "Beth, I have a surprise for you," he said.

She smiled uncertainly. "That sounds mysterious. What are you talking about?"

"How would you like to stay in your own home to work for me?"

"You mean I could take manuscript pages home to type?"

"Better than that. I'm going to buy you a word processor and have it tied into the university computer. We'll hook up a telephone line with a set of earphones so you can stay in touch and discuss the chapters with me as you type. When you've got my garbled manuscript in order, you can type it right into the computer and it'll be printed out, with copies, right here."

She sat down abruptly. "You're kidding."

"No, I'm not. You're the best helper I've ever had, and I have no intention of losing you if I can help it. I'm afraid you'll worry so much about those kids of yours that you'll quit."

"Will the university allow such an arrangement?"

"Sure. I'll be renting the computer time from them as an independent. The arrangements are my own prerogative."

She leaned back in her chair, smiling broadly. "Wow, that will be having my cake and eating it too."

"There's a slight catch, though."

"Uh-oh," she said, amused. "You want me to be on call twenty-four hours a day."

He laughed. "Nothing so crass as that. But I'll have to ask you to do a little more of the slave work if I invest in computer time. Up until now you've done only my textbook work. I've been paying another woman to prepare my lessons. It's only part time. She's about to leave for North Carolina to take a full-time job, and I'd have to find a replacement in the fall. It isn't much, a few hours a week at the most, and the computer will make it easy. The catch is, I'm asking you to do those few more hours of work, and I can't really pay you much more for them since I have the expense of the setup."

"But that isn't much of a catch," Beth replied, excited once again. "There have been times when I felt guilty about you paying me when I couldn't do much but keep quiet while you struggled with a way to explain a principle to me. And besides, I can get a good hour's work done in the time I'd have spent commuting each day. I won't have to worry about taking the bus or replacing my old car or buying any more clothes."

Tim laughed indulgently at what she realized had been an ingenuous response. "Then it's okay with you?" he asked.

"Oh yes, I'm delighted."

"I'll have to spend a little time late this summer getting the thing set up in your house and teaching you to use it."

She smiled broadly. "Oh, Tim, I can't thank you enough."

"Just do me one favor," he said. "If you and Joe don't get back together, give me a chance, okay?"

She stood up and gathered her purse and a potted plant from her desk. "I think this arrangement may make it a little easier for us to get back together, Tim," she said softly. "But even if we don't, Joe Columbine is the only man for me . . . ever."

He smiled ruefully. "Have a good summer, Beth."

Joe arrived at Springfield Realty the following Monday morning to learn that Mr. Springfield had invited the entire staff to lunch that day. As each staff member arrived, incredulity and speculation grew. In all the years Joe had been working for Springfield, the old man had never splurged like this.

146

Joe watched him surreptitiously. He hadn't been looking very good since that long bout of flu in early May. Maybe it had mellowed the old slavedriver.

Besides himself and Mandy, the staff consisted of old Mr. Bill Miller, who, at seventy, was nearly as old as Mr. Springfield; Tom Barrick, twenty-five and the father of year-old twins, hard-working and optimistic; and middle-aged Susan Weller, a widow with a handicapped child who supplemented her commissions by working as a secretary in the office.

At noon they all walked the three blocks to the restaurant, where they were met by George Jr., who was sitting at a private table for seven. That was even more of a surprise than being invited to lunch, Joe thought. The younger Springfield was thirty-seven if he was a day, but as far as anyone knew, he'd never done anything more useful than serving as president of the Countryside Country Club. They seldom saw him around the office unless he wanted money from his father. He'd been photographed last summer for having hit two holes-in-one in one season. His florid good looks were rapidly going to fat.

He was sitting at the table, nursing a manhattan and wearing an aggrieved air. As the staff filed to the soup-and-salad bar, Joe noticed the waitress substituting a full glass for an empty one in front of Sonny, as the elder Springfield called George Jr.

Joe smiled wryly. It was a mystery to him how Springfield, who could be such an unmitigated tyrant with the people who worked for him, could be such a cream puff where this worthless son was concerned.

When they'd nearly finished eating, the elder Springfield tapped his glass with his knife for attention. As if there were seventy of us instead of only seven, Joe thought contemptuously. The man was unbearably pompous.

147

"Ladies and gentlemen, I'm sure there's been a great deal of speculation about the reason for this impromptu treat," he said with a mirthless smile. "I'm not one of those social-butterfly businessmen."

Understatement of the year, Joe thought. He noticed that the others were watching their boss warily, well aware that something momentous was about to be announced.

"Well, folks, I won't keep you in suspense any longer," the old man continued. "I'm going to step down as president of Springfield Realty."

Joe felt his mouth drop open and shut it quickly. He saw similar reactions, as well as an almost joyful incredulity, on the faces of all the staff members. Nobody uttered a sound.

"Doc says that bout of flu in May took its toll," Springfield was saying. "Left the heart a bit damaged. Damn foolishness, I say, but Maudie's laid down the law. She wants to be a wife, not a widow, she says. So Sonny's going to be your new man at the helm."

The office staff seemed to catch its collective breath. Sonny frowned and gulped down the contents of his glass. He made a gesture with his right hand as if acknowledging applause, which acted as a signal to old Mr. Bill Miller, who led a bewildered and desultory round of clapping.

Joe was at once depressed and elated by Springfield's news. He also had a strong impulse to hug Maudie, Springfield's plump but browbeaten wife. Imagine her being that concerned over the old tyrant's health. She was a good old soul. But George Jr. looked miserable. She must have put the fear of God into him, too.

When everyone had expressed concern for Springfield's health and congratulated him on his good sense in retiring, they all went back to the office. Springfield told Sonny to be there in an hour, and the younger man nodded glumly. To Joe, he murmured that he wanted to talk to him privately.

Wants to be sure Sonny's got a nursemaid, Joe thought cynically.

He proved to be right. After giving him a lecture on loyalty to one's employer and saying, rather uneasily, Joe thought, that of course he never for one moment expected anything less from him, the old man made his pitch.

"There's bound to be a bit of confusion when a new man takes over, Joe," he said. "I know I can count on you to do all you can to help Sonny learn the ropes. He's going to need coaching to pass his real-estate examination next month and to run the business."

Joe waited, not speaking. The old man was watching him nervously.

"Of course, there'll be a new title and a tidy raise for you. Can't expect you to take on additional duties without recompense, now, can I?"

Joe held his peace.

"How does Joseph Columbine, Office Manager, with a three-thousand-a-year raise grab you?" Springfield said blusteringly.

You're getting a hell of a bargain for three thousand, Joe thought angrily. Sonny will be as useful as a snowball in Alaska. I'll be running the firm single-handed. Not that he hadn't been doing far more than a simple employee for years, he thought bitterly. But there was the mortgage and the kids and his hope of persuading Beth to stay at home. The three thousand would more than pay her tuition. He nodded, unsmiling.

There was a quick flicker of relief in the older man's eyes at his acquiescence. He smiled and extended his hand.

Yes, you barracuda, you've got me for now, Joe thought with resignation. But maybe not for much longer.

"Let's go introduce the new office manager to the staff," Springfield was saying jovially.

Joe nodded again and followed his boss to the outer office.

9

Beth's final check for the work year plus the bonus Professor Ternan had happily added brought her bank balance to more than eight thousand dollars. She realized, of course, that there would be income tax to be paid on the money when they filed their return. Still, it was a sizable amount.

When Joe came home from work, he headed straight for the kitchen, where she was preparing dinner. She looked up as he came through the door, smiling broadly.

"You look as if your horse came in," she said teasingly.

"In a way it did. Guess what? The old man's retiring."

"You're kidding!"

"No, I'm not. Seems the flu left his heart damaged, and for once Maudie's put her foot down. Made him hang it up."

"Good for Maudie. And, oh, Joe, good for you, too. I think," she added, watching him uncertainly. "He isn't going to . . . to . . . dissolve the firm, is he?" Even as she asked the question, she thought it might be the catalyst that would get Joe thinking about a firm of his own.

"No, Sonny Boy is to be the new president. Nominally, of course. I'm to be office manager, and he's given me a raise. Of course both Springfield and I know who'll really be running the operation," he said with a touch of bitterness.

He sank down at the kitchen table and loosened his tie, unbuttoning the top of his oxford cloth shirt.

"That wimp," Beth said contemptuously. "How's the old man going to get him off the golf course long enough to be

151

president, even nominally?"

"Frankly I wish he'd stay out there. It'd be a lot easier running the business without having to conduct the sham that he's the head of it," Joe said grimly. "At least I'll be indispensable."

"I'm not so sure of that," she said dolefully.

"Come on, Beth, can you imagine George Junior running the firm?"

"No, I can't. But suppose he surprises everyone. Or suppose a nephew or someone else shows up. They'd dump you without another thought if they didn't need you. Right now, you're a necessary expenditure, like the computer was. If he could see a way of making money without you, he'd let you go."

"I've always known that. But where would he get anyone else to work for what I do, even with the raise?"

"Then, knowing that, I think you ought to consider quitting."

"Are you insane?" he cried, almost angrily.

"The entire operation would just collapse without you." She watched him, understanding his anger.

"Beth, honey, that's easy for you to say," he said patiently. "If you quit, things would go on pretty much as usual. But I have to have a job. Where would the house and car payments and the food we eat and the utilities come from if I weren't working? A family man can't just quit a good job for the hell of it!"

"Not for the hell of it, Joe. To start a business of your own." She got up quickly and walked to the stove, not meeting his eyes. She stirred the spaghetti sauce.

"A business of my — Good Lord, Beth! You've been out in the sun too long."

"Or you could offer to buy Springfield out."

He gave a bark of mirthless laughter. "Buy him out? What

would I use for collateral to get the money? My castle on the Rhine? How about my Ferrari? Or my stock portfolio. You know damned well the market's been down for a couple of years because of interest rates."

"And doesn't that strike you as pretty rotten, Joe? You told me once that you *know* more than half the clients in the firm were brought in by you, yet he's paying you as if you were just a salaried employee. How many times have you told me you wish he'd at least have a profit-sharing plan?"

He shrugged. "That's the way it is for a family man. You can't have everything in life."

Beth gazed at him warmly. "You've paid for putting me and the kids first, haven't you, Joe?" she said softly.

The lines in his face eased as he met her eyes. "I've never begrudged the cost, Beth, you know that. You and those wonderful kids — hell, nothing on earth is worth more."

"Just the same, the sky would have been the limit for you if you hadn't had so much baggage through life."

He rolled his necktie absently into a coil, not answering.

"Joe, I'm serious about trying to start your own business or trying to buy out Springfield," she said hesitantly. "What would it cost to acquire his firm?"

He flattened his hands on the table and sighed in an elaborate show of exasperation. "Well, supposing he was interested in selling a golden goose, I'd imagine he'd want at least fifty thousand dollars."

"That much?" She was temporarily daunted. Then she smiled. "It doesn't sound so bad. You could borrow most of it."

"But we'd have to have a sizable down payment. We'd need more money than we're ever likely to accumulate."

"Would twenty-five thousand be enough of a down payment, do you think?"

153

"Might be. Times aren't good for borrowing money. Interest rates are high. And it's a marvelous firm. Sound as a nut. But we'd never get our hands on that amount of money."

"We've got it, Joe. We do!" she said at his startled look. "Oh, not all in cash, but we have to have thirty-five thousand dollars worth of equity in this house. And . . . and . . . we've got eight thousand dollars in the bank, too," she added all in a rush.

"We don't," he said in disbelief.

"We do. I asked Mr. Holm at the bank today what he thought our house would be worth on today's market, and he told me. It's really appreciated since we bought it, Joe, and you've always paid ahead on the mortgage."

He waved that away, although she could tell he was impressed. "We don't have a bank account," he said doggedly.

"Wait." She withdrew her passbook from her purse and spread it out at the page that showed the balance.

He stared at the figure in disbelief. "You mean you've been earning enough to make those kind of deposits?" he said dazedly.

"I've been getting nearly a thousand a month, and my boss gave me a bonus for working this summer so he could meet his deadline. He says I've earned every cent of it, too," she said proudly.

"I'm happy for you, Beth." He pushed the book toward her. "But this is your money, not mine."

"Then the house must be yours since only your money went into it, but my name's on the title," she snapped. "I'm trying to tell you, this money is ours, Joe, just as the house and car and furniture are ours."

He stared at the checkbook almost wistfully.

"The money is only a symbol, though," she persisted. "Don't you see? For months I've been trying to make you understand

154

that I can make a real contribution. I can bring you more money, of course, but also the confidence I'm gaining in myself can only enrich our marriage."

He shook his head stubbornly. "I just can't accept it, Beth, and I'm sorry. I still can't see how your working and studying has enriched our marriage. What good does it do us to have more money, even to buy a real estate firm, if we've grown apart? And we've fought so bitterly. I feel you going your own way in life."

She scarcely breathed. The words he was saying were the same old stubborn words, and she could feel his anguish as he said them. Yet there was a hesitancy, too, as though he was no longer quite certain.

She thought incongruously of the day they'd gazed at the rainbow arching across the sky. Cindy had said she'd never hate rain again if it was responsible for bringing the magical vision in the sky. Beth felt like that now, as if the storm in their lives was about to end and a more brilliant, beautiful world take its place. She longed with all her heart to overcome Joe's fears, to rush in as she had so often in the past with quick reassurances of her undying love and devotion. She felt that the way she answered him now would make a profound impression on him.

"I'm not convinced we've been drifting apart, Joe," she said slowly. "Oh, we're not living together. We've only slept together once in three months. We're self-conscious about even talking together, as we never used to be. On the surface, yes, it appears that we've been growing apart. But during these weeks when we've been trying to find a way to live with this impossible separation, we've worked together and respected each other as we never did before. I think you've noticed it, too."

He had been listening attentively. Yet Beth felt he wasn't ready to cross the last barrier of acceptance. He reached out and covered her hand with his, a sad smile on his lips.

"Joe," she said gently, "next year I'll be working from the study upstairs instead of at Professor Ternan's office. Although I'm not capitulating to what you want, it's going to be a lot nicer for me. I hope you'll be pleased."

He smiled in delight. "I can't pretend I'm not happy to have you out of that wolf's office, but how are you going to work it?"

She told him briefly about the computer console and telephone headphones Professor Ternan was willing to install. Joe nodded as she talked.

"You never had the least thing to worry about," she teased. "What woman in her right mind would be interested in Tim Ternan after having had Joe Columbine?"

He smiled with pleasure and turned her hand over, planting a lingering kiss in her palm. Beth felt the shock of it clear at the base of her spine. She shivered convulsively and withdrew her hand, dropping it into her lap. Joe watched her with tender eyes.

"Don't trust yourself, Valentine?" he murmured seductively.

In answer she grinned and thrust her tongue out at him.

"Right now we have to discuss business," she said, growing serious. "What about buying it?"

He sobered, too. "I admit I haven't given much thought to our equity in the house," he said slowly. "And I didn't know you had so much money. If I did need it, though, I'd insist it be only a loan."

She started to interrupt him, but he raised his finger to her lips. She subsided. They could argue mine and thine later, she decided.

"The fact is, people who have money know how to hold on to it. And that firm *is* money. These old moneyed families aren't about to sign away the family castle."

"But if the mortar that's been holding the family castle

together suddenly lets go, they'll find themselves living in a shaky pile of rocks," she said swiftly.

Joe stared thoughtfully at his coiled necktie. "I see what you mean," he said slowly. "They might prefer having the castle's value instead."

"Exactly."

"We could talk to someone at the bank," he said with cautious hope.

"It wouldn't cost anything to talk to someone," she agreed happily.

"I'm a damned good credit risk. As you pointed out, I've always paid ahead on the mortgage."

"You had the babies paid for before they were born." She smiled, remembering how Joe had divided the doctor's fee into seven parts and insisted she take that amount to her obstetrician each month when she went for her checkup. By the time the babies had been born, the O.B.'s fee had been paid.

"It isn't a good time to float a loan. The interest rates are high," Joe said thoughtfully.

"On the other hand, the stakes are high," she said, acting as devil's advocate. "Even with the interest rate, you'd receive all the firm's profits and not just part of them."

"They're out of sight, too, even with the recession," he said. She could see that he was controlling his enthusiasm for the new idea with difficulty.

"And best of all, you'd be ensuring your future in the profession you love."

He frowned suddenly. "We're assuming an awful lot, Beth," he said. "Maybe Springfield will fire me for even suggesting he consider selling to me."

She was instantly indignant. "Then you just tell him you're resigning," she said with spirit.

"Do you realize what you're saying? What the hell will I do

if he accepts my resignation?"

"Start a real estate firm of your own," she said steadily. "I know it won't be easy. But you already have your broker's licence. You're only thirty-four years old. You're in a better position to make a break now than you'll ever be again. Think what it would be like to be, say, forty-seven and have George Junior drop a bomb on you. Your options would be considerably limited then. We can do it together, Joe, I know we can. I don't make a great deal, but it would keep body and soul together until you can get your own firm established. And it would mean so much to you to be your own boss."

"It would be pretty hard for a while."

"I like working. It's been so exciting, learning how a book goes together. You know I've always wanted to write." She paused shyly. "I don't think you were paying much attention when I told you, but I even have a novel outlined and the first draft of an opening chapter completed. I'm planning to send a query letter to a publisher soon."

He stared down at her, smiling. "I was paying attention, and I'm proud of you. I'm sorry I didn't say so then. Hon . . . Beth, I'll be able to pay your tuition with the raise I got. I was ashamed to tell you before, but I didn't think I could afford to pay it."

She stared back, her face stricken. "Oh, Joe, you crazy guy. Why didn't you tell me that in the beginning?" she cried. "You let me think you were just being selfish and nasty!"

"Would it have made any difference?"

"Of course. I would have understood."

"But you'd have still gone to work to earn the money."

"I did anyhow," she pointed out reasonably, "and it caused so much bitterness." She shook her head. "Anyhow, right now we have to talk about this business proposition. Let's talk to Mr. Holm at the bank."

Joe threw his necktie over his shoulder with an air of determination. "Okay. Get Jenny to baby-sit and meet me downtown at one. If I can't get the appointment at that time, I'll call you."

Joe sat in the office of the vice president of the bank, Beth at his side. His stomach felt as if it were doing pushups. He explained to Brad Holm that he wanted money to make an offer on Springfield Realty.

"Let me get this straight, Joe," Brad said, filling his pipe. "George Springfield is retiring and putting young George in his place as president of Springfield Realty. He's naming you office manager. But you'd like to make him an offer to buy his firm instead."

"That's right, Brad."

"And you'd like us to advance you the money, using your wife's savings and the equity in your house as down payment."

Beth stirred slightly. "The bank account isn't only mine, Mr. Holm. I just haven't been able to talk Joe into signing the slip giving him access to it."

The banker acknowledged her remark with a nod. "You feel the firm is worth perhaps fifty thousand dollars and that's what you want to offer."

Joe nodded again. The banker leaned back, grinning and puffing on his pipe.

"I'm sure Springfield ought to be pleased with such an offer since everyone in town knows you've been head honcho there for a long time. But what makes you think he'll go for it?"

Joe met his gaze steadily. "Because if he doesn't, I'm going to resign and start my own firm. Beth has convinced me there's no reason under the sun I can't do it. I already have a broker's license. But I'd prefer working from the same location, hiring the existing staff."

"I think your wife's right."

Joe smiled proudly. "She usually is."

159

Mr. Holm puffed thoughtfully on his pipe. "Would you mind taking some advice?" he asked.

"Not at all."

"Well, I'd have to clear it with the board, of course, but I don't think there'd be any problem about giving you enough money to purchase a controlling interest in the firm. Why don't you talk to Springfield about a partnership? You could include a clause that would allow you to buy him out, say, in ten years. He won't last much longer than that, I'm sure, and I'm also sure he realizes his son won't be able to hold on to the business alone. It would give him time to put his capital in trust for his son. I think he realizes he blew his opportunity years ago to make a man of George Jr. A deal like this would be tailor-made for him to look after his son's future."

Joe and Beth exchanged glances.

"It sounds like a good idea," Joe said. He looked as though he'd just taken a hurdle he'd never quite expected to master.

"Of course, this is all off the cuff, you understand," Mr. Holm hastened to add. "You don't need to quote me." He stood up in gentle dismissal and shook hands with them. "Talk to Springfield, Joe, and let me know how you make out. And I wish you the best of luck in negotiating with him. I know you'll make a success of the firm."

During the next few days their excitement reached burn-out proportions. Beth invited the Springfields to dinner on the following Saturday night. She and Joe went together to shop for groceries, taking the children along and stopping afterward for a sundae at the Felicity House. Beth had planned the dinner carefully, deciding on a simple antipasto tray, lobster bisque, lamb roast with spicy glaze, green bean casserole, and pineapple ice with Chinese almond cookies. It would be a lovely meal.

Joe stood in the front hall, gazing through the opened sliding doors into the big dining room, two bags of groceries in his arms.

"Do you realize we're risking all this?" he said in a tight voice. "We could lose our home."

She lifted her chin proudly. "We could lose our *house*. The *home* has been gone for some time now, at least the way we always thought of it."

His dark eyes bored into hers. "It's not gone, not yet," he said.

She couldn't bring herself to give him the response she knew he wanted. She turned and led the way into the kitchen through the front hall doorway and started putting groceries away.

"Do you realize how insane this is?" he said, putting the bags down on the table. "Here we are, inviting people to dinner as a couple, planning a joint business venture that will tie us together for better or worse for the rest of our lives, and we're separated."

She laughed. "It does seem a little strange, I guess," she said lightly.

He grinned winningly. "You really can't get along without all the excitement I provide, can you?"

"I sure don't want to," she conceded.

He moved closer and cupped her face in his hands. "Do you want me to come all the way home?" he whispered.

She gazed up into his eyes for a long time. Much as she wanted to, she couldn't see there what she was looking for, his acceptance of her as a true equal in the marriage.

"I think it would be a mistake," she said with a sigh. "I'm just not convinced it wouldn't be just sweeping our differences under the rug."

"Everyone's got a little dirt under the rug, honey."

She shook her head. "Not me. God help me, I have to have what I thought I was getting in the original transaction. And I think you do, too, if you're to be permanently happy."

"Why do you always make everything so complicated, kitten?" He sighed and kissed her eyelids. "I so want things the way they used to be, I can't stand it."

She stood motionless, her face still cupped in his hands, gazing at him silently. At last he sighed and stepped back. "What do I have to do to get you back?"

She shook her head, ashamed of her own confused uncertainty. "I don't know, Joe," she said at last. How could she explain the sensation she'd felt growing, the feeling that she was watching for some sign? "I honestly don't know."

On Saturday evening, Beth put on a white silk dress and pearl earrings. She slipped her stockinged feet into white kid sandals and dabbed English lavender behind her ears and between her breasts. She added a coral lip gloss that highlighted her early tan, then started downstairs to check on dinner.

Joe came down from the apartment as she reached the upstairs hall. He was so good-looking in a cream-colored sports jacket and medium-brown slacks that she found herself staring in admiration. She ached with longing at the mere sight of him.

"How do I look?" he asked, smiling.

"Gorgeous," she said simply.

"You're beautiful, Beth." He smoothed a curl, smiling wistfully.

Reluctantly, she led the way downstairs. They had fed the children and settled them in front of the television set upstairs, having told them that it was a business party and that their parents needed to concentrate on their guests tonight.

Beth reached for her apron and checked the roast and bisque. Joe gently tied the strings, then turned her back to stand in front of him. He leaned down and kissed her gently.

"Whatever happens, I'm grateful for your encouragement.

162

Do you realize what we're doing? Do you? You stand to lose in this, too."

"I'll worry about it later. Right now I have to baste the roast."

She checked the progress of the other dinner items. When the doorbell rang, she removed her apron, throwing Joe a look of camaraderie. "Count five and then answer it," she said breathlessly.

He went to admit the Springfields as she carried the hors d'oeuvres into the living room.

The elder George Springfield was a short, wiry man with thinning hair and sharp gray eyes. He'd always made Beth nervous. His wife was a gentle-faced, rather pretty woman shaped like a plump pear. She seemed completely immune to the baleful effect her husband had on his associates. George Jr. looked like a playboy. When he shook Beth's hand, she smelled mouthwash and a whisper of whiskey that it didn't quite disguise. His gray eyes darted elusively. He was sunburned and overweight.

"It's very nice of you to invite us to dinner, dear," Mrs. Springfield said brightly. She eyed Beth's antique platform rocker and, to Beth's relief, sat on the couch instead. Mr. Springfield chose the place beside her. George Jr. handed Beth a bottle of Chianti and sank down on the green armchair.

"Since you're Eye-talian, I figured Chianti would be the ticket," he said bluntly.

Beth thanked him, trying to smile. She loathed Chianti but hated even more the assumption that they'd like it because they were Italian.

She allowed only fifteen minutes for appetizers and chitchat. The meal was ready, and there seemed little point in extending the cocktail hour.

The Springfields seemed to enjoy the food. Beth noticed

that Joe ate mechanically. She could scarcely swallow a mouthful. Their guests apparently thought the dinner invitation was a thank-you for Joe's new position, and they referred to it often, paying little attention to the amount she and Joe consumed, much to Beth's relief. She felt like the fly who'd invited the spider into her parlor, and suffered a momentary pang. But as she observed the arrogant Mr. Springfield and his empty-headed son and thought of how Joe had slaved for him, more than doubling his business, her doubts vanished.

At last they withdrew to the living room with snifters of Grand Marnier. Joe met her eyes and squared his shoulders. His employer asked for an ashtray and lit a cigarette without asking if they minded.

"Yessiree," he said, inhaling deeply, "I'll bet you never expected to rise so high, Joseph. Not every Eye-talian kid fresh out of college gets a break like you did, finding a spot in an old, established firm. Not that you haven't repaid my confidence. Didn't I always tell you the boy repaid my confidence, Maudie?"

Mrs. Springfield nodded dutifully and reached for a chocolate mint. "You sure did, G.R.," she said pleasantly. "You said if you wanted anything done and done quick and right, you told Joe to do it and it was as good as done."

Beth glanced at Joe, who was smiling woodenly. Her heart turned painfully as she realized anew what he'd had to endure from his insensitive employer. She met her husband's eyes and smiled, trying to put her love and encouragement into her expression.

Joe's dark eyes acknowledged the message. He turned purposefully to Mr. Springfield. "Sir, I'd like to discuss the changes in the firm now that you're retiring. I don't think I can go along with the plans you've outlined."

Springfield withdrew his cigarette and glared at Joe. "You're not about to try to hold me up for more money, are you?" he said harshly.

Joe returned his gaze steadily, shaking his head. "This isn't about my salary, Mr. Springfield." Beth could hear restraint in Joe's tone. "At this point in my life, I'm concerned with my future. This seems a good time to take stock of it."

"Boy, you've got a good future as long as you stay with Springfield Realty," said his employer with a bluff goodwill that didn't match the wariness in his shrewd gray eyes. "I s'pose, like most of us, you're worried about money. Inflation and all that. Must take a nice bit of change to keep up a big old house like this. But without me at the helm, now, and Georgie not knowing the business yet, the firm might suffer a bit at first. Still if you're in need of more, I might see my way to allowing you another thousand a year."

Joe shook his head again. Beth noticed a pulse beating furiously in his neck, but his demeanor and voice were completely relaxed.

"No, I'm sorry, that's just not the problem. Your leaving has been just the catalyst I need. You see, Beth and I have a little capital, and I think the time has come for me to strike out on my own."

Springfield's mouth dropped open. His mustache quivered under his aquiline nose. He was no more astonished than Beth, who hadn't expected Joe to quit before he attempted to negotiate. She knew how a person marooned on a desert island might feel as he burned his life raft. Still, she kept smiling. Her blood was racing, and she felt curiously exhilarated.

"Strike out! My God, what the hell are you thinking of?" Springfield thundered. "Georgie can't . . . that is, I was counting on you to mind the store and teach my son the ropes."

Joe smiled gently. "I am sorry about that, sir," he said with a regretful shake of his head. "In fact, that's why we invited you all to dinner. We just wanted to say thank you for the offer. I learned the real estate business in your office and grew to love it. I wouldn't worry about your son. Like as not, he'll prove to be a chip off the old block and surprise you."

Beth had never realized Joe was such a good bluffer.

"Hell, Daddy, you told me I wouldn't have to do anything but hire and fire and you'd come in to help me with that!" George Jr. interjected, looking thoroughly alarmed. "I don't know one damned thing about the real estate business, and I'm not about to learn either."

"Sonny, just calm down, dear." Mrs. Springfield shoved another mint into her mouth, licked her fingers, and put a restraining hand on her son's sleeve. "Daddy will get it all straightened out. It'll just take a little more money than he figured on."

"Shut up, Maudie," Springfield snapped. He turned to Joe with an air of strained patience. "Let's just lay our cards on the table, boy. What do you want?"

Beth had to remind herself to breathe. She kept her eyes riveted to Joe's expressionless face.

"What do I want?" Joe put his glass down slowly and met his employer's angry gaze. "I want my own firm, Mr. Springfield, and I'm going to get it, too, even if I have to start from scratch. It'll take me a while, but I don't think it will take me forever. I have a very strong feeling that many of my clients at Springfield Realty will want to do any future business with me wherever I work. Yesterday I worked out on the computer how many of them I personally added to your firm, sir. The figure astounded even me. Do you know what percentage it was?"

Springfield's face was impassive, but his eyes darted fire.

"It was sixty-three point four percent, Mr. Springfield," Joe said quietly.

"I don't believe you!"

"I don't lie, Mr. Springfield, but I'm not asking you to believe me." He pulled the computer printout from his pocket and held it out to the older man.

"Daddy, he can take them all away," George Jr. snapped.

Joe ignored the outburst. His dark eyes never left his employer's face. Mr. Springfield took a handkerchief from his trouser pocket and mopped his forehead.

"What do you want?" he said gruffly. "I'll give you ten thousand more a year."

Unexpectedly, Mrs. Springfield turned and scowled at Joe. "George hasn't been well. You've got no call to upset him."

Joe regarded the woman compassionately. "Mrs. Springfield, I'm aware that your husband hasn't been well, and I'm truly sorry about that. I'm not harassing him for more money or anything like it. I told him honestly that I want my own business. I'm prepared to offer him a business proposition that will be beneficial to all parties. Just bear with me."

"Business proposition?" Springfield said cautiously.

Joe nodded. "Beth and I have considerable capital and can borrow more. We're prepared to start a real estate business in Bellemonte. We would have a few lean years, but then I'm sure we'd prosper. My prosperity would very likely harm you since, as you pointed out, George Junior doesn't know the business yet."

"And I have no intention of learning it either," George Jr. repeated with a defiant glance at his father. He drained his glass and reached for the liqueur bottle.

"Exactly," Joe said, unperturbed. "Now, rather than following that course, I'm willing to offer to buy fifty-five percent interest in Springfield Securities with an option to buy the other forty-five percent in, say, fifteen years. If George Junior truly has no interest in the business, he needn't even show up. If he changes his mind and wants to learn it, I'll willingly teach him everything I know."

The elder Springfield snapped his jaw shut and stared at his son, who was trying to stifle a belch and looking relieved at being freed from the necessity of going to work.

"What would you be willing to pay for a fifty-five percent interest, and what would the terms for the later acquisition be?" he said quietly.

"Thirty thousand dollars," Joe said promptly, "which is, I'm sure you know, a generous offer even if you don't consider that I personally wrote well over half the clientele. At the end of the specified time, whatever we agree upon, I will buy out the original forty-five percent, excluding, you understand, the new accounts I'll have added, at the prevailing market value, whatever it may be."

Beth's heart was fluttering wildly. Steady, Joe, steady! You're doing fine. I think you've got him.

The old man stood up, his shaggy brows knitted together. He gave an unexpected bark of laughter. "Well, boy, damn it, you're a sharper business man than I ever gave you credit for," he said almost reluctantly, but with an edge of admiration in his voice. "There's just one thing I want to ask you about. It's common knowledge that you and your missus have been having problems. I was reassured to get the invitation from the two of you. Fact is, I was considerably worried about offering you the position of office manager because of the . . . irregularity of your domestic arrangements. Isn't that so, Maudie?"

She nodded dutifully. "But you had no choice," she said helpfully.

Her husband glared at her. Joe had trouble suppressing a smile.

"I guess you've got a right to ask, Mr. Springfield," Joe said. "I give my word that the problems between my wife and me are of a minor nature, and we're working on them. Whatever

168

happens in our personal lives, we'll honor our business commitments, and we're both prepared to incorporate that promise in any contract." He smiled at Beth.

The older man nodded shortly. "Well, then, on Monday morning we'll get started on drawing up the papers." He had the air of a man who had expected to be executed and, instead, found himself conducted to an island paradise. He smiled and thrust his hand out to Joe. "Well, partner, looks like we're forming a new firm. Springfield and Columbine."

Joe took the old man's hand and gripped it firmly, smiling broadly. "Columbine and Springfield, sir," he said.

Beth almost burst out laughing at his cheekiness and the expression on Mr. Springfield's face.

10

The rest of the week was a veritable whirlwind for Beth as they wrapped up the details of the partnership and prepared to attend the wedding of Joe's brother.

On Friday Joe took part of the day off so they could get an early start to their parents' homes. In his pocket was a newly purchased stock with options to be given as a wedding gift to John and Liz, although Cindy maintained they'd like the hound puppy named Bashful better.

Beth was aware that, if not for a nagging, unverbalized hesitancy on her own part, she and Joe would have been completely back together.

Why can't I just accept him back? she asked herself as she packed. Why did she have a persistent conviction that, despite their growing oneness, the basic rift between them was still unresolved?

She asked the children, as straightforwardly as she could manage, not to mention their problems to any of the relatives since to do so would only give pain and worry to them at what should be a happy time.

"That's all over now, isn't it, Mom?" Josh asked, staring at her with his father's eyes.

"I hope it will be soon, sweetie," she said, too honest to lie to them, despite an overwhelming desire to reassure them.

They arrived at Joe's family home at four in the afternoon. Joe grinned as he pulled into the curb. They could hear happy bickering and laughter even on the street.

"Clan's gathering," he said to Beth.

His sister, brother-in-law, six-year-old niece, grandmother, and several aunts and uncles were in the second kitchen his parents had installed in the basement. His father, a twenty-years-older, twenty-pounds-heavier, pewter-haired version of Joe, sat smiling at the head of the table as Joe's mother, beautiful and vigorous, served cold Italian meats and pastries. Beth fondly watched her mother-in-law's enjoyment of feeding people she loved. From the amount of food on the table, you'd never have suspected there was a caterer slaving down at the Union Hall on Green Avenue or a sumptuous rehearsal dinner waiting at the Italia Restaurant for the wedding party and the parents of the bridal couple.

"Eat. Eat. *Mange, bambini,*" Joe's mother was saying. "*Ci vuole un po' di carne sull'osso.*"

"What's that mean, Grandma?" Cindy asked, munching on a Danish.

"It's nice to be a little plump." Her grandmother smiled and pinched her cheek. Cindy giggled.

"We stopped for pie about an hour ago, Mom," Beth said doubtfully.

"It's just a bite to hold you until supper," said the older woman.

"Oh, you mustn't worry about supper for us. We know you have the rehearsal dinner to attend," Joe said.

"I'm not worrying. Beth's mother has been making pizza and antipasto all day. She told me when she brought some cookies she baked for the reception. She was getting beds ready for the children, and your father was buying Popsicles." She lifted a pot of coffee from the stove, using her apron as a hot pad, and poured cups for them. "You two will sleep here, though," she said decisively. "In Joey's old room."

Beth could feel Joe's eyes on her. They should have discussed the sleeping arrangements. How could she get out of sharing a bed with him now? In spite of herself, the thought of sleeping next to him — and maybe making love — made her heart pound with excitement.

When Joe's father asked him how things were going at work, Joe took a deep breath and told them all about buying into the firm. Beth recognized a new confidence in him, an indefinable air of being in control that must have reassured his father, who nodded and raised his eyebrows as if impressed at Joe's explanation of what a sound move he was making.

Maybe Joe wouldn't need to dominate her now that he was in control of his own life, she thought suddenly. She realized she'd just had a flash of insight about their relationship. Suddenly she felt vastly encouraged.

"Hey, Joe, you're a big shot!" his sister Consuela cried, giving him an affectionate slap on the arm. "Next wedding, you'll probably be driving a Lincoln."

Although obviously pleased with her teasing, he looked a little shy, too, as though he hadn't quite assimilated the magnitude of the change in their lives. Beth prayed silently: *Let it be right, God. Let it be right for us. I can't express what I mean, but You know.*

Joe retrieved their suitcases from the car and carried them up to his old room.

"Get your bathing suit, Dad," Joe called. "Grandpa Mateo will have filled the swimming pool by now."

Beth's parents lived only three blocks away. They'd put in a pool for when Beth's and her sister's children visited.

Joe came downstairs carrying Beth's two-piece royal blue suit and his maroon trunks along with their matching terrycloth cover-ups. His mother handed him a house key.

"In case we're not home yet when you're ready to go to bed," she said.

"Oh, it's so hot, we'll probably stay in the pool till late," Beth replied, unaccountably breathless. Joe smiled enigmatically. She knew he was laughing at her behind the smile.

His mother shrugged. "So maybe we'll be in bed before you get home. Take it, you can let yourself in."

A few minutes later, Beth's parents greeted them warmly and encouraged them to eat again. Beth's mother was tiny and quick with iron-gray hair and hazel eyes. Her father was tall, lithe, and quiet. He loved books and plays — any kind of drama or fiction — as much as Beth did. They would be attending the wedding, too, since the families had been friends for years.

After supper, they sat on the screened patio, talking. Joe told them about the partnership and the children asked if their grandparents would like a puppy. They leafed through the family photograph album, laughing at the pictures.

It was nearly dusk when the family went swimming. The pool had been fenced to keep out unsupervised children and unleashed pets. Thick, beautiful evergreens planted all around the fence gave the entire back of the house, pool, and patio an attractive privacy. Beth put on her bathing suit in her mother's powder room and blushed as she went out to the pool where Joe was waiting, warm appreciation shining in his eyes.

"You're the most gorgeous, sexy, desirable woman I ever saw," he murmured, glancing at the others to be sure they didn't hear. "I want you, Beth. I want to run my hand across your bare stomach."

She moved quickly out of earshot, her senses clamoring. He was absolutely devastating, his muscled body relaxed and glistening as he stretched out on a chair beside the pool.

The tension grew between them as, a few minutes later, they slipped into the pool. Even the splashing and racing of the children did little to distract them from their well-concealed preoccupation with each other.

The children's bedtime passed, and they begged to stay up a little longer, since it wasn't every day they got to swim in the dark. Beth didn't need much coaxing. As long as the children remained, she wouldn't be alone in the dark, in the sensually warm water with Joe. Yet at the same time she longed for just that.

Finally Beth's mother called the children inside.

They clambered out of the pool, shivering. "We don't have to take baths, do we?" Josh said.

"There'll be too much confusion for you to have baths and shampoos in the morning," Joe answered.

"We'll take care of everything," Beth's mother assured them. "I'll help them bathe and shampoo. Might as well get the chlorine off."

"Grandma, we don't need help," Cindy said with dignity, clutching her arms and shaking like a leaf.

Little by little, the children and their grandparents disappeared inside.

"Turn off the light, Ma." Joe called as his mother-in-law shooed the last child through the door. "We'll be going over to my house soon."

"Okay, we'll see you tomorrow at church." She switched off the light.

Joe and Beth were left in near darkness, only a distant street lamp and a few stars allowing them to see each other dimly. Sudden silence enveloped them. Beth saw her husband's dark shape gliding slowly toward her in the water.

"Joseph Anthony Columbine, I —"

He lunged forward and grabbed her, drawing her into his arms and effectively stopping her comment with a kiss. It was not gentle. He gave the melodramatic laugh of a stage villain, his mouth still tightly against hers.

"Well, me proud beauty, I have you in my power at last," he said theatrically.

"Joe, please, please let me go. Oh, I knew all day this would happen," she said, both distressed and powerfully aroused.

He took her lips again, more gently this time, his hands sliding down her body, holding her captive.

"Don't, Joe." She tore free from his lips, treading water, trying to get away. He gripped the front of her bathing suit bottoms and began untying her top. She felt it floating up between them, secured only by the tie at the back of her neck. His hands moved around her body in unison, cupping her breasts. She moaned and tried to pull away. "Someone might come out," she cried softly.

"No, they won't. Your parents aren't *that* old," he whispered in her ear, "and we could be in the Canadian northwoods with that forest your father planted. Makes you wonder what they've been up to, doesn't it?"

He pulled her closer still, kissing her deeply, bending her head over his hand at the back of her neck. With the other hand he drew her hips against his body. Beth was trembling with desire. She clung to him to keep from drowning, knowing that if he stopped treading water, she'd be too weak to support herself. He released her neck and pulled her to a shallower spot where they could find a foothold. Beth felt her feet touch bottom, and Joe turned her to envelop her again. His kiss forced her mouth open. She felt as if her whole being, heart and soul and body, was open for his love.

"I want you. God, Joe, I want you," she gasped.

He was kissing the line of her jaw, her ear, her neck. He lifted her straight up out of the water and buried his face between her breasts, his breath sizzling on her wet body.

"Let me go, let me go."

"No, Beth, I won't let you go. I've had about all I can stand of letting you go," he murmured. His mouth was moving on her breast, almost burning her. Slowly he let her down into the water, his hand moving to the elastic of her bathing suit bottom. "The water's a great aphrodisiac, kitten." He laughed softly. "Let's install an indoor hot tub."

He noticed all at once that it wasn't just the love play that was causing Beth's body to shake. She was crying. He smiled tenderly. She always cried when she was deeply moved.

"What's wrong, baby?" he asked gently, kissing her.

She put her head on his wet shoulder, slumping in defeat. "How can you torture me like this?" she sobbed.

"My intention wasn't exactly to torture you," he said patiently. "I'm just making love to my wife. I'm trying to show you in the most straightforward way I know that I want to resume our marriage."

"It isn't right, Joe. It just isn't right."

"Not right to make love with your husband? I *am* still your husband."

"Would you ask me to marry you now, knowing what you know? That I'm a feminist, a liberated woman, that I have a mind of my own and go my own way?"

He hesitated only a split second, but it was enough to confirm her suspicion.

"You're beautiful and kind and dear and good," he said. "You're a great wife and a wonderful mother. I'm lucky you even looked at me. Yes, I'd weigh all that against your independence and still marry you."

She pulled away from him and made her way to the edge of the pool. "You didn't have to weigh anything when you married me," she said unhappily. "It's not the way we thought."

He followed her. "Beth, you can't leave me now. My God, we're both almost ready to go into orbit from tension. Do you want me to have a seizure and drown?"

176

She shook her head, trembling. "I'm sorry, Joe. I didn't start this, you did."

"I've had just about all I intend to take of this nonsense," he said ominously, pulling her back into his arms.

"What are you going to do about it, Joe, rape me?"

He stared down at her dim outline in the water. She tried to get the suit decently across her breasts. "Don't cover them, Beth. You're so beautiful. You look like a water sprite. A lorelei . . . we've got to have some answers, Beth. We're in a marriage, for better or worse. We've been acting like a well-matched pair in every way except that you're denying me your bed. Isn't it silly to hold out on me this way? On yourself?"

She shivered uncontrollably. She felt cold in the night air. Her heart felt cold, too. Joe's cynical, pragmatic arguments depressed her.

"I have to admit it does seem silly," she said dully. "It isn't that I don't want to make love with you."

"Then, why not? Maybe we haven't got all the answers about our marriage yet. All I know is, if we both don't soon have a release from this tension, we'll be basket cases. We promised each other for life, although we've forgotten that lately, it seems. You act as if having sex with me would be immoral. If it was someone else, it would be immoral. But I'm your husband!"

"That's the most depressing mishmash of theology and hedonism I've ever heard," she said wearily. "I can't help the way I feel. And I feel that having sex with you, marriage or not, would be immoral under the circumstances. I am not the woman you thought you married; you've admitted that. I never, never dreamed I would want a divorce until I wanted to go to school and all this . . . all our different perceptions of our marriage came out into the open. You keep calling me a feminist as if it was a dirty word, but the truth is I'm not a modern feminist. I'm very old-fashioned and traditional. I just can't make love only to release the tension. To me, our lovemaking was always a powerful, jubilant affirmation of our oneness, of our *marriage.*"

She turned away and began climbing out of the pool.

Joe pulled her gently back. He tied her bathing suit top and almost reverently kissed her bare back.

"All right, Beth. All right, darling," he soothed. "You don't have to do anything you don't feel is right. Come on, I'll walk you back to my parents' house." He clambered out of the pool and helped her up. "Then I'll come back over here and sleep in the camper."

She gulped and nodded. "What will I tell your parents in the morning?"

"Tell them it got too hot, and I came back for a swim and to sleep outside," he said with a wry grin. "That's not far from the truth."

He put her terrycloth jacket around her shoulders.

"Joe, you're a good man, and I love you," she said gratefully.

"Yeah. But haven't you heard? Good guys finish last."

Nevertheless, once Joe had seen Beth safely inside his parents' house, he smiled to himself on the walk back to her folks' place, though his body was throbbing with desire, and he probably *would* take another cold swim.

Had there ever been a woman like Beth? The most strict confessor would call her scruples inordinate. He'd loved her for a long, long time, but even he hadn't understood the strength of her principles. The notion of sex for recreation or self-gratification was simply beyond her comprehension. When she said "making love," it wasn't a euphemism; she meant it quite literally. What happened between them was holy to her, like the sacrament of marriage itself.

His beautiful wife wouldn't play the strumpet for any man.

Not even him, he thought proudly.

178

* * * * *

Joe sat with Beth and the children in a pew just behind his parents. The organist struck up the processional and the congregation stood, watching as Liz walked slowly down the aisle on her father's arm. She was small and full-breasted, and in her peasant-style dress she looked young and lovely. Behind the concealing veil she was smiling radiantly. Joe glanced at his brother, who was waiting with his attendants at the altar, and saw the same joy in his face as he watched his bride coming toward him. Joe's eyes dimmed.

Get a grip on yourself, man, he admonished himself. Everyone expected the women to get teary-eyed at weddings, but they'd laugh at him for a fool if they knew.

He realized it was Beth's face, not his prospective sister-in-law's, that he was seeing above the white dress. Beth had been the most beautiful woman he ever hoped to see, her big, dark eyes shining with love for him, her luxuriant brown hair piled beguilingly on her small head, the delicate lace of her mantilla framing her heart-shaped face.

Had he considered Beth his possession, his chattel, his subordinate on that day long ago? Had he honestly believed there was an unspoken contract between them that said he would be the master? He felt an overwhelming sense of confusion as Liz's father drew the veil back from his daughter's face and kissed her before placing her hand in John's. He was assailed by a sense of déjà vu. Had he received Beth from her father's hands as if she were a piece of property? Had he?

He could remember nothing but the overwhelming happiness of that day. He'd felt himself the most fortunate man on earth.

Gently he took Beth's hand. She smiled up at him, dabbing her eyes with a tissue. They looked a little red-rimmed, as though her weeping last night had left its mark. Her simple rose-coral dress gave a tinge of color to her face, but still she seemed wan to him. He had been grieving her greatly. He'd always cared about her needs — until this past year when her needs had seemed to clash with his. When the stress of caring for three toddlers had showed on her pretty face, he'd picked up the telephone and called Jenny or her predecessor, her older sister Georgette, to come look after their babies so he could take Beth out for dinner or just for a ride. Then Beth had remembered that she was a woman as well as a mother, and her eyes had sparkled for him again. He smiled tenderly in recollection.

"Memories, sweetheart?" he whispered.

She nodded and, as they knelt for the beginning of the nuptial Mass, she leaned close and whispered in his ear, "I was remembering our third date."

He grinned, acknowledging the shared memory. By the third date he'd known he loved her. He'd taken her to a stranger's wedding. They'd slipped quietly in the back door and knelt as the marriage vows had been exchanged and the Mass completed. As the bridal couple had come striding joyously down the aisle, Joe had urged Beth to look at their faces. "Don't they look happy?" he'd said, and Beth had known he was trying to propose.

She was gazing tenderly at him. When his brother and his new wife turned away from the altar and faced the congregation, she echoed his words of that day. "Don't they look happy?" she whispered. Their eyes held in silent understanding.

At last, the wedding party arrived at Union Hall, where the caterer and his assistants were laying an enormous, L-shaped, tulle-hung table with a veritable banquet: roast beef, ham, chicken, rigatoni and meatballs, small pigs in a blanket, potato salad, fresh garden salad, fresh strawberries and melon, and trays of cookies from the aunts' and friends' kitchens. The

Italian wedding cookies looked like miniature Easter eggs of many colors; the "clothes-pin" cookies were incredibly delicate pastry baked around clothespins, then filled with the lightest of creams; there were also date and crumb bars and chocolate-chip cookies. As the guests filed in, the caterer's helpers carried in colorful gelatin and fruit concoctions and turned on the champagne fountain.

In the opposite corner of the big hall a bar had been set up over which Joe's uncles now presided.

Beth, Joe, and the children passed through the reception line, giving and receiving hugs and kisses. Joe's mother, vividly lovely in flamingo-colored chiffon, and his father, smiling in spite of the unfamiliar tux, introduced them to John's new in-laws. Joe hugged his younger brother and new sister-in-law exuberantly, then presented the envelope with the stock certificate.

"It's good stock, Liz," he murmured. "Maybe by the time you and John settle down it'll help make the down payment on a house."

John seized it and clapped his brother on the back. "Hey, Papa," he cried, "your oldest son's a hotshot owner of a realty firm and your youngest a lawyer. What do you think of that?"

Joe's father smiled broadly. "That's nice. I'm proud and so's your mother. We got two fine men."

Joe and Beth hugged his parents again and moved down the line. "Oh, Joe," Beth murmured, "it's good to be here."

He drew her hand through his arm as they chatted with old friends and more relatives. The children ran off with their cousins. The orchestra struck up a waltz, and Joe drew Beth onto the dance floor. She drifted gently into his arms, fitting there perfectly. She belonged with him, he thought ruefully, but how could he convince her of that? Maybe his possessiveness — yes, call it what it was, his chauvinism — had

181

already ruined his chance.

Joe danced a polka with his sister and his mother then once with John's bride, but the rest of the evening he held Beth in his arms.

"It's the only way I can get you here," he said whimsically.

When the bride and groom were circling the hall saying their farewells before their departure, they stopped to chat with them for a few minutes.

Joe's great-uncle Tony, exuberant from the occasion and a bit more whiskey than he was used to, stopped and embraced them all. He put a chubby arm around John's shoulders and one around Liz's.

"Hey, Johnny, you shoulda come by the house to talk to your uncle Tony last week. Never mind, I talk to you now. How's it feel to be a married man, huh?" He squeezed John's shoulder, laughing with good humor. "You don't know yet, you tell me next week when you get back from wedding trip! You gonna like, I tell you." He rolled his eyes comically. Liz blushed, but smiled indulgently.

"You gotta pretty wife, Johnny, but you better take a stick to her quick, so she don't get no funny ideas about who's boss. Put a baby in her belly quick and see she don't fool around getting supper ona table. None of this lady lib stuff."

To Joe's complete astonishment, an almost overpowering anger gripped him. He remembered receiving shatteringly similar advice from his great-uncle Tony at his own wedding reception. Had he been influenced by it? Had he really taken values of the Old Country so much to heart?

He realized that the orchestra had stopped and that most of the wedding guests were observing Uncle Tony's lecture with amused interest. Beth was a small, quiet presence beside him.

"John, if you have any sense at all, you won't listen to a word he says," Joe thundered solemnly. "Good Lord, a woman's not a horse or a dog or a cow!"

Uncle Tony's mouth sagged open in astonishment. He looked at Joe as if to be certain that he really was his great-nephew. Joe was acutely aware that all the wedding guests had fallen silent and were watching. Beth's gaze, wary and disbelieving, was riveted on his face.

"I don't mean to be disrespectful, Uncle Tony," he said. "You're my godfather and you bought me my first grown-up suit. I love you. But things are different now." He paused, groping for a way to put into words the hard-won truths he'd learned.

"What's this, 'different'?" Uncle Tony said skeptically. "*Your* wife had a baby . . . three babies in three years. You the bosso!"

"No, Uncle Tony, I'm not the bosso. I'm the husband. Beth's the wife. I'm the man, she's the woman. Two. Two parts of a whole. Equal. She stands beside me. Beside me, Uncle Tony, as smart and capable as I am. What good is a woman to a man under his heel or his thumb? It's better to have her in his arms." He paused and stared down at his wife, whose eyes were sparkling, lighting up his whole world. "Next to his heart," he added.

The entire assembly broke into delighted cheers. Beth was laughing and crying all at once. Still, she didn't move toward her husband. She waited, watching for the sign to be complete, waiting for the rainbow at the end of the storm.

Joe took both her hands in his and raised them solemnly to his lips, ceremoniously kissing the back of one, then the other.

His dark eyes met hers, beseeching her to understand the gesture. She did. It was the Italian symbol for deep respect.

"I love you, wife. With all my heart, soul, mind, body, strength, and honor," he said solemnly. "In the presence of God and this company."

She couldn't see anything but his dear shape for the tears of joy in her eyes. He was saying he loved her in front of all these people. He loved her as an equal, a true partner.

At last the sign had come. Like a benediction from heaven. Like a rainbow. Joe saw that her reservations were gone. He opened his arms, and Beth went into them, close to his heart.

Their children cheered and encircled them in a tight embrace. Joe smiled down. "You kids can stay with Grandma and Grandpa Mateo for a while, but Mommy and I are going home."

The children clapped their hands and ran off. Joe drew Beth closer. "Come on, darling. We're going swimming again."

Despite the crowd of delighted onlookers, Beth brought her lips to his and kissed him without restraint, pouring all her love into the embrace. When finally they pulled apart, her face was glowing. "Yes, Joe, oh yes, with all my heart, yes," she said.

Joe clasped her hand tightly in his and strode purposefully forward, pushing a pathway through the crowd. Several uncles and male cousins clapped him good-naturedly on the back, congratulating him and urging him on. Beth couldn't contain her happy smile or take her eyes off her husband. The orchestra struck up another exuberant polka, and several couples began dancing with gay abandon as voices rose to a crescendo.

At last they reached the door and stepped outside, standing breathless in the sudden silence. Their eyes locked in an intense gaze, their expressions turning serious, their hearts too full to speak. Hand in hand, they began walking. They left the celebration behind, hastening to their own celebration, to the reunion for which they'd long struggled, hoped, and dreamed.